HIDEAWAY

HIDEAWAY

Eloise McGraw

A MARGARET K. MCELDERRY BOOK

ATHENEUM   1983   NEW YORK

LIBRARY OF CONGRESS CATALOGING IN PUBLICATION DATA

McGraw, Eloise Jarvis.
Hideaway
"A Margaret K. McElderry book."
Summary: When his father forgets to come for him
after his mother leaves on her wedding trip with her new husband,
twelve-year-old Jerry runs away from both of them to his
grandparents' house, only they don't live there any more.
[1. Runaways—Fiction. 2. Divorce—Fiction.
3. Remarriage—Fiction.]   I. Title.
PZ7.M1696Hi   1983   [Fic]   83–2786
ISBN 0–689–50284–2

Published simultaneously in Canada by McClelland & Stewart, Ltd.
Composition by Maryland Linotype Composition Company
Baltimore, Maryland
Printed and bound by Fairfield Graphics
Fairfield, Pennsylvania
Design by Christine Kettner
First Edition

To Dan and Robbie

HIDEAWAY

ONE

He found the street about dusk—7:42 by his birthday watch—on a clear blue day in early September, the worst day of his life.

Not just the second-worst, Jerry thought as he halted beside a big windblown cedar to stare toward the house. The *worst*. The one that was going to change all the other days to come, whether he liked it or not, whether anybody liked it or not. At least this time the change was going to be *his* way. He'd made up his mind.

He forced his tired legs on, only to stop again after a few steps, still peering toward the house. That *was* the house, wasn't it? Must be. His memory hadn't played him any tricks so far. Once past the confusion of the Portland bus station, where he'd hung around nervously for a long time making sure of where you got your ticket, how you found your bus—once on board at last, and headed coastward down the Sunset Highway, he'd pretty much known he could do the rest. He'd been back here to Horseshoe Beach only once since he'd lived in Portland—only one lousy half-day in five years—and even that was a long time ago. But they'd come on the Greyhound that one time, he and Mom, and he remembered exactly how they'd got to this street. You crossed the highway two blocks beyond the Crab Pot Cafe, where you got off the bus, and that was Pelican Avenue; you followed that a long way to West Tenth, then turned toward the ocean and crossed White Heron Road. Then up the hill to White Heron Place and down to Gull Street and the next hill was Sandpiper Road. He'd remembered because of all the bird names. And here he was, right where he'd expected to be, staring at the fourth house from the corner on the crest of the hill.

In the old, gone days when he and Dad and Mom lived just down the coast in Fisherman's Bay, he'd spent half his Saturdays right there in that house. It was bound to be the right one, whether it looked exactly as he remembered it or not.

All the same, it wouldn't do any harm to wait a while. Let the dark close down a little.

He glanced around. Not a soul in sight. He walked back to the big wind-twisted cedar, unslung his school backpack from his shoulders and tossed it under the broad, low branches. Then he crawled underneath himself, found a spot near the trunk relatively free of twigs and prickles, and leaned back, slowly letting every bone and muscle in his body undo until he sagged against the rough trunk as limp as a worn-out pillow. That was just what he felt like, too, a worn-out pillow. Only not so comfortable.

Not so—*finished*, either.

He sat up straighter, folded his arms, fixed his eyes on the house. He wasn't finished at all. He had things to do yet and he could do them. He'd got this far.

A door slammed, somewhere farther along Sandpiper Road. Otherwise the place was quiet, as though nobody lived here. Of course you could always hear the ocean, booming and rustling and swishing away in a steady undertone, though it was out of sight beyond the row of houses, and way down below. Now that he was listening, he could hear sea gulls crying, and the evening breeze beginning to fret its way through the dense, scratchy spiral of limbs above him, even cars whisking by now and then four blocks away on West Tenth. But no kids yelling or parents calling them in—not even a TV sort of voice, though there were lights in some of the houses, so there must be TVs—and people.

Maybe they were all old people, or anyway sort of old, who didn't make much noise about living. Like his grandparents.

Automatically his glance went back to the house. It was dark and empty-looking. That was all right, that was as it should be. They were away. They wouldn't be back till—when? September eighth or ninth, Gran had said. Right after Labor Day. Anyway, after the baby was born. And this was only September second.

As he watched, a light went on in the house. Jerry jerked upright. *Two* lights, one in the far corner of the downstairs, and one in a little side window upstairs.

Were they *there*? Already? Oh . . . if only they were *there* . . . He was halfway out from under the tree before a doubt stopped him. Would it be good or bad, if they had come home early? His father was their son, after all. They might be on their own son's side. And he hadn't seen them—except that one hour or so last week—for five whole years.

He wished they could have stayed around longer last week. Just one lunchtime wasn't half enough after all that time—and his father had done most of the talking, grownups always did. What's more, there'd been a baby at the next table—closest to *his* chair—that kept yelling and banging its spoon and drowning out whatever *anybody* was saying. If Gran and Grandad had been his mother's parents, instead of his father's, he bet he'd have seen them lots more often during those five years. As it was, he'd barely begun to get acquainted again when lunch was over

4

and they were gone. He could only hope they were the way they used to be.

Slowly Jerry sank back, still staring at the two lights. For the first time he wondered if he should have come. What if nothing worked out the way he hoped—the way it *had* to? Everything would get lots worse than it was already.

So what did he do now? Were they really home? Those lights looked too dim to be doing anybody any good. They looked like the single lamp you left on somewhere when you were going to the movies. Still, he'd *seen* them turned on—both at once, as if somebody upstairs and somebody downstairs had . . .

Then he got it. They had a couple of those gadgets you hook up before you leave for somewhere, that turn a light on when it starts to get dark and turn it off a few hours later. Elton Brook's family had one.

He sat a moment longer, just breathing, swallowing the lump again, letting his insides get back to normal, letting all the adrenalin and stuff calm down. As you were, he told himself. They're still gone. They won't be home for a week or so. And meantime nobody knows where you are, they all think you're somewhere else. Everything's the same.

It was dark enough now to get moving. Nothing to be scared about, he told himself as the tingling started up again in his fingers and toes. That's Gran's and Grandad's house and *they won't mind*. He took a firm grip on the straps of his backpack and struggled out from under the drooping branches.

Slipping across the dusky street, he shivered suddenly, and wished he'd brought his jacket. His pack held nothing warmer than a long-sleeved knit shirt. Back in the city it had been a hot day—hot enough for swimming, as he had reason to remember. But the Greyhound had carried him over a mountain range since then. Here at Horseshoe Beach it was always cooler than inland. It got nippy as soon as the sun set, and mornings were damp and cold. He might have remembered that from the years he'd lived on the coast himself.

He'd found the right house. The closer he got to it the more certain he was. Beyond it he could make out the looming mass of the row of huge hydrangea bushes that screened the far side of the yard from the little public pathway down to the beach. And there at the near corner was the Climbing Tree—a big Sitka spruce with twisty, wind-bared branches spread so wide and low that even a really little kid, as he had been once, could scramble all over it. As near as he could tell in what dim light still lingered in the sky, plus a bit from the streetlight just coming on at the corner, plus the blurred, golden shine from that single lamp behind the living room curtains, everything was the same.

So what was it that kept seeming a little different?

Rubbing his arms below the short sleeves and swallowing again, he peered uneasily at the dim

6

lines of window frames and shutters, the horizontal stroke of the little roof that ran across the front of the house. He used to think it looked like a long black eyebrow over the living room windows, with the nose the front door—he remembered that. The eyebrow wasn't black now, though. The gathering dusk made it hard to see colors but he thought it was red. Maybe *that* was all—they'd repainted the trim of the house. That would make it look different, wouldn't it? The rest seemed the same as always: weathered cedar siding silvered like driftwood. The windows on this end would be the kitchen, which seemed perched high because the land dropped away underneath, so that the breezeway deck next to it had to be on stilts and the carport—half visible behind the Climbing Tree—on a different level from the breezeway, several steps down from it.

All remembered, all as it should be. But the last time he'd stood here, looking, on that single visit from Portland, he'd been seven years old. Now he was twelve. Five years. It seemed a hundred years. It seemed like somebody else's life, back then. In a way, it was. The little wind brushed him with chilly fingers, bringing up the gooseflesh.

I won't be cold in the house, he told himself. If I can get in.

He started toward the far side, where a walk stepped down the slope between the house and the hydrangea bushes. He'd planned hours ago to try the playroom door first; that latch never wanted to hold

7

even when the night lock was on. The door was warped, Grandad always said. It was hard to get to but if it wasn't any worse than it used to be, he could do it, all right. He pushed his way past the stiff, rustling branches of the hydrangeas, letting them slap to behind him, smelling the green, juicy smell of the bruised leaves, careful of his footing because the walk ended somewhere here in a crumble of rock and broken concrete, unless they'd fixed it. He found it by skidding on it perilously, grabbing at the hydrangeas and finding them intertwined with blackberry, full of thorns. Time to use his flashlight, if he could get it out of his pack in these close quarters. He sucked the little torn spots on his hand, and flapped it up and down rapidly a few times, then, much hampered by blackberry and darkness, worried the pack around far enough to thrust a hand in. As he drew it out grasping the flashlight he heard a man laugh, so close on his right side that he went clammy all over.

"Oh, I doubt that," said the same voice that had laughed. "I doubt that very much. Unless she was only kidding. Old Stan—"

"She *wasn't* kidding, I was *there*." A woman's voice, soft and rapid, broke in and went on, yakkity-yak, proving things and quoting people until it had receded out of earshot.

Jerry stood weak-kneed, swallowing repeatedly.

Just some people coming up the little path on the other side of the blackberry tangle after a walk on the beach. Only five or six feet away—but they couldn't have seen or heard him. Thanks to the trouble he'd had getting at the flashlight. If he'd already turned it on could they have seen the flicker? Sure they could've. Bound to. So did he dare turn it on now? For all he knew, a dozen other people might be coming back from walks—whole families —all the neighbors on the street. Maybe that's where everybody was.

He blinked into the darkness, shivering, trying to decide. But there was no choice, really. It was turn it on or break a leg.

Shielding the working end of the light with his right hand, he pushed the button, and was relieved to see what a small circle of gravel and weeds was illumined at his feet. It was only a two-dollar flash after all—not much bigger than a penlight. Cautiously but as rapidly as possible he made his way down the slope, half sliding, clutching at ferns and horsetail grass, with the little golden circle dancing from one foothold to the next among the roots and rocks.

Then he was down, and safely beyond the bushes at the corner of the playroom. Nobody could see a flashlight here, unless it was somebody on a ship at sea. Beyond the retaining wall yonder there was nothing but air and ocean, with a steep rough embankment tilting to a ribbon of sand thirty feet below, and a flight of wooden steps snaking down to it.

Following the flitting light along the strip of grass

between wall and house, he bounded up the three weathered steps to the lower deck and the playroom door.

And this time—of all times—the latch held firm. He tried all the tricks Grandad used to use to test it—lifting as he pushed, bearing down and banging his shoulder against it. It was as solid as if it were nailed shut. Maybe it *was* nailed shut. Maybe Grandad had decided that was the only answer. Nobody had ever used this door much anyhow.

So it was time for the big gamble. He played the light over the big window beside the door, but he knew it was the fixed kind that didn't open. All the ones that did were casements, and would be locked tight, with the winding-handles taken off. He'd watched Grandad doing that in the old days, just for the short trip down the coast to Fisherman's Bay to take him home, after he'd been to visit them. They'd have done it for sure before this two-week absence.

That left one answer, as he'd known even before he left the bus. This, Jerry thought without amusement, was where he found out how much he'd grown in the last five years.

Switching the light off now, he moved silently on across the deck and up the stair at its far end, around the other corner of the house and up another four steps to the narrow-roofed breezeway deck that connected the house and carport. Straight ahead in the darkness should be the back door, leading into the kitchen through a right-angled passage Grandad always called the dog room, because he kept old Bingo's water dish over beside the freezer, and fed him there. Old Bingo was long gone, but . . . Jerry switched on the flashlight, shining the golden circle straight on the door. The dog-door was still there, set into the lower panel.

So far, so good. He drew a long, uneven breath of relief strongly tinged with doubt as he snapped off the light. Bingo had been a big dog, but that rectangle looked a lot smaller than he remembered. Of course, he'd been a lot smaller himself when he last tried this. For a seven-year-old it had been easy enough. The best he could hope for now was not to get stuck half in, half out, and have to yell until someone came.

Humiliation rushed over him at the very thought. I'll never do *that*, he thought. I'd rather starve.

Without letting himself imagine any further, he unslung his backpack, eased the flashlight through the hinged panel onto the dog room floor, and leaving his arm inside up to the shoulder, began trying to work the rest of him in too.

It took him fifteen minutes, half a dozen trials and failures, and a collection of scrapes and bruises. Twice he came near panic, thinking he really was stuck fast. But he had grown far more in length than in breadth; once he had disjointed himself enough to get head and shoulders through, the rest of his string-bean body followed, delayed only by his belt-buckle hanging up maddeningly on some obstruction just where he could not reach a hand to free it. Somehow he bounced it loose, punishing his vertebrae and ribs on the top of the opening, then the hard-edged door-square was rasping along his jeans, catching and holding his crisscrossed, bulky shoes until he frantically scraped one off. He heard its muffled thud on the deck outside as he slithered at last onto the dog room floor and lay gasping and spent on the cold linoleum.

He was in.

Slowly the realization spread and blossomed. He was in. He'd done it. He was here.

And now that he'd made it, he was never going back. Never.

He never wanted to see his father again. Or his mother either. All they cared about was *their* lives, and what *they* wanted, never about what it might be doing to him.

He was going to have his own life now. From this night on.

The linoleum was hard and slick, with a suggestion of sand that he remembered. No matter how you swept, Gran used to say, you could never get rid of the sand in a house near the beach. It was chilly, too. Jerry hauled himself up from the floor, staggering a little in the darkness, and groped around for the flashlight. He was feeling as tired as if he'd run all the way from the city. Tired and—empty, somehow, instead of triumphant.

Maybe he really was empty—hungry. He'd had

nothing since that restaurant omelet hours and hours ago, at which he'd nibbled without tasting it . . . He shied away from the thought of that hard-to-swallow meal, the agonizing hour that came after it.

Recovering the flashlight, he unlocked the back door, brought in his backpack and discarded shoe, and reset the night lock behind him. Wriggling his foot into the shoe, he opened the cupboards, one by one, shining his little circle of light over canned goods and cleaning stuff and paper towels and empty fruit jars. Where had Gran moved the peanut butter? Maybe the refrigerator, though she never used to keep it there.

He moved on into the kitchen, careful to keep the light below the level of the counters until he could close the woven-wood blinds on the windows over the sink, which faced the street. Even then he decided against turning on a light—the flashlight was plenty.

He found the peanut butter in the refrigerator, along with a few possibilities for tomorrow, and—after a real search—finally located the crackers in a drawer. *Weird*, he thought. Who ever heard of keeping crackers in a drawer? He used a knife from the rack beside the sink to spread a stack of them with peanut butter, and leaned there in the dark, devouring them, and trying to remember where Gran used to keep them in the old days. Surely not that drawer, but he couldn't precisely visualize them in some other place. It bothered him, he didn't know why.

Of course there wasn't any milk or anything. Jerry went through cupboards again until he found a glass, drank some water, and put the glass in the sink with the knife. Then on second thought he went back and washed them both, and dried them and put them away. Crackers back in the drawer, peanut butter back in the refrigerator. He didn't want to make a big mess in Gran's and Grandad's house—they wouldn't appreciate that.

They might not let him stay.

But they *had* to. They would. He knew they would.

He slung the backpack over one shoulder and left the kitchen, silent on his thick rubber soles, stopping short in the dining room doorway at sight of the very last of the sunset—a long dramatic crimson streak where sea and sky met, drawn all across the dark dining room and west living room windows, the width of the house. It was a moment before he noticed the small, regularly repeated gurgling noise, like a single bubble of air being loosed under water and then bursting on the surface—like a pump? He stood very still and listened. Eventually, by the sound and by a dim radiance coming from some-where out of sight at the other end of the living room, he located its source: a large, glass-sided box stand-ing in the far corner of the living room win-dow seat. A fish tank! So that's what Gran and Grandad had got to take old Bingo's place. It seemed a puny substitute. Jerry started across the end of the hall toward it to take a look, but stopped short of the archway leading into the living room. The dim light that fell on the tank must come from a lamp in the front window—the one he'd seen from across the street. It would light him, too, if he walked past that partition. Better not go in the living room at all until tomorrow. He swung sharp right instead and bounded quietly up the stairs, two at a time.

The upstairs light he'd seen was the one in the little bathroom at the south side of the house, next to the guest bedroom he'd always slept in. Handy to have the light, so long as he avoided making shadows on the blind. But it was a Venetian blind now, he discovered by peeking in cautiously—a new one. Pink. *Pink?* Gran was always saying she hated pink. Unless he was remembering wrong. Maybe she thought her guests would like it. Or maybe she'd changed, but Jerry couldn't believe that. It would be so nice, he thought with sudden urgency, it would be so *great*, if only Gran herself could be here, instead of just her house.

At any rate, Venetian blinds wouldn't show shadows like Gran's old ones. Feeling uneasily visible all the same, he used toilet and washbowl, hung the towel up, and got out as quickly as he could. He was beginning to feel as if today had been going on for most of his life, and would probably go right on forever. I'll turn in, he told himself. All I need is some sleep. I won't feel like this tomorrow.

He groped his way into the little guest room, switched the flash on, then off, just to be sure they hadn't moved the furniture. But they had. There was a little couch where the bed used to be. A few more cautious probes of his light—this room was at the front of the house, over the kitchen, so he dared not turn on a lamp—showed him a desk, a small TV. It wasn't even a guest room any more, but a kind of den. Disconsolate, he stood wondering what to do. He didn't want to sleep in Gran's and Grandad's own bedroom, it didn't seem right—and it was the only other room up here. Why did they have to change things? He hadn't realized till now how much he had been longing for the little old-fashioned bed and yellow-striped curtains, and the wallpaper with a pattern like chicken wire, that did funny three-D things when you unfocused your eyes. At least the wallpaper was the same—and the bookshelves built in to the corner. Oh, what did it matter? Everything in the whole world was different anyway, so why not this?

He swung out of the room again, blundering painfully into the door jamb in his haste to get on with it, to quit standing there feeling as if the sky had fallen. He supposed there would still be blankets in the linen closet—there was no different place to move those to. He found an old-looking plaid one, and a pillow, dragged them back to the dinky little couch which was barely long enough for him, and

16

flung himself down on it any old way, kicking off his shoes and pounding at the pillow as if he hated it. He did hate it. He hated everything, he hated today, he was going to hate tomorrow, he hated what he had done, he hated being way down here alone and cut off, with his bridges burned. But most of all he hated the new life that would be coming if he had stayed where he was.

No, most of all he hated Dad. *How* could Dad have yanked the rug out from under him again? *This* time? Other times—well, it hadn't mattered quite so much, or he'd still had enough give left in him to see Dad's position, anyway put his own aside. But you could give and give just so long, then all at once the give ran out, and that was *it*. Even with your own father. You'd just *had* it. For good and all.

A wave of misery washed over him as he clutched the old plaid blanket, turned his face into the pillow, stiff-armed his emotions. Forget it, forget it! He told himself fiercely. But all the desperation and resentment and raw hurt held at bay till now by the need to plan and act was bunching up in his throat in an aching knot. And finally he quit trying, and let the storm burst.

TWO

◆◆

At 10:05 Monday morning, Hanna drove Barney Cotter's old jeep down Sandpiper Road to the house beside the big Sitka spruce. She turned in, swung right around the angled driveway, and halted just short of the carport. Switching off the engine, which gulped and bucked convulsively as it subsided, she sat a moment whistling, gazing out the driver's-side window toward the ocean. She was thinking about herself. It was a subject that occupied a large part of her time and attention—possibly because it had occupied very little of anybody else's in all her sixteen years.

Just now she was considering her name. Holderith. Hanna Holderith. Actually it had a sort of nice sound. Almost an aristocratic sound. It was German, she supposed. Or Austrian, that was better.

18

Maybe her father had been an Austrian count, on a diplomatic mission to western Oregon—no, scratch that. He was on a ski trip to the Cascades, and fell desperately in love with this little waitress at Timberline Lodge—a pale, fascinating girl with curly red hair . . . Hanna's glance met her own skeptical green eyes in the rear-view mirror. Scratch "fascinating," too. Well, maybe this waitress (or ski-instructor or whoever) had been dark and beautiful, and *he'd* been the redhead—this Austrian count (or truck driver or visiting millionaire). It was a sure thing one of the two had been pale, and freckled, with curly red hair, and *plain*. Plain, plain, plain.

And sturdy. Mustn't forget that, Hanna cautioned herself as she climbed out of the car. She could still hear Mrs. Murchison's high, whining voice—a musical-saw kind of voice: "Hanna's a plain child, but she's sturdy. I will say that." And she *had* said it, oh, how often, as she sat overflowing that old greasy flowered chair watching Hanna lug out the garbage or wrestle the even younger foster kids into their high chairs. My first compliment, Hanna thought flippantly, unlocking the back door. Ten years old, still waiting for somebody to say something nice, and then I didn't appreciate it.

The trouble was, being told you are plain but sturdy made you feel like an economy-model vacuum cleaner, and at ten years old she had still wanted to be a princess. Not any longer. All she wanted to be now was solvent, so she could get out

19

of foster homes forever. Not that the Cotters were so bad, she begged their pardon. Best of the lot, in fact. Especially their son Barney, who at twenty-two sometimes took her back forcefully to herself at ten. But the whole scene was yuk.

She tossed her purse onto the counter, then wandered on past the dining-L into the living room, whistling, hands in her windbreaker pockets, eyes fixed on the ocean. You could hardly look anywhere else, in these rooms that were all west windows— that expanse of sapphire blue out there caught your gaze and held it. Sapphire blue this morning; green yesterday; battleship gray all last week, with fog rolling and shifting; and she'd even seen it flat and no-color, but still you couldn't quit watching. And that window seat running the width of the living room, inviting you to just sit and stare. She wondered if the goldfish appreciated their million-buck view. It would be great to live in a house like this— peaceful, uncrowded, nothing skimpy or mark-down or make-do or the wrong color or garishly brand-new, but just comfortable and quiet, as if it had all been rubbed and polished and touched a lot.

She turned her back on the ocean, walked to the front door, unlocked it, and went out to get the mail. Nothing there yet. Monday morning—mailman probably running late. That suited her fine; she'd wait for him. Samantha would probably say leave it till tomorrow, bring in the haul for both days together. But Samantha didn't need to know.

Smiling, Hanna went back inside, scattered the gold-fish's dandruffy-looking food on the surface of the water and watched them flash up to get it. Then she went into the kitchen to fill the watering pot.

It was then she spotted the crumbs—a sprinkling on the side counter, a few on the floor. Cracker crumbs, they looked like.

Funny. She'd never noticed them till now, and she'd been coming here every day for a week and a half. But they must have been here whether she'd noticed or not; *she* hadn't been eating any crackers, and how could anybody else get in? There were dead-bolts on all the doors except the back one, to which only she and Samantha had keys. If she'd checked the window locks once she'd checked them half a dozen times. All the same, she was almost willing to swear . . .

She *was* willing to swear it. On Saturday she'd over-filled the watering pot and had to mop this very counter. The crumbs had appeared *since then*.

Funny nothing, she thought, with an unpleasant little chill running over her. Downright peculiar.

She found she was standing rock-still, the water-ing pot clutched in both hands, listening so hard she could hear her ears ring. There wasn't anything else to hear, except the fish tank burping, a dog barking down the street—probably at the mailman—a dis-tant truck grumbling along on Tenth, and of course the ocean, murmuring under everything. There was nobody in this house except her and the fish—as she was now going to prove to herself by going straight through it, into every room.

Carefully she put the pot on the drainboard, turned and marched across the corner of the dining room then turned right up the stairs. In spite of herself she was keeping her movements silent; realizing this, she began to make as much noise as the stair carpet would allow, and after wetting her lips twice she managed a breathy whistling. Give them time to hide if they could, whoever it was. All she wanted was to find nobody.

There was nobody to find. Nothing. Just peaceful, empty rooms. Hall with phone and windowseat. To the left, the little den and bath; to the right the owners' airy, sun-filled bedroom, plus another bath with baby-blue plumbing fixtures, and on the side toward the street, a storeroom.

Hanna relaxed a little. There couldn't be anybody here. Still puzzled but a lot less nervous, she went downstairs, doubled back along the hall to the other flight of stairs directly under the first ones, and a moment later stepped warily into the single big basement room—the art room or whatever it was. It, too, was filled with sunlight from a wide west window. It, too, was empty, except of course for the two presses and the clutter of sketchbooks and pencils and pens and bottles and tubes and gouges and glue and rags and a million other things scattered over the long worktable and the makeshift counter beside the sink—and on the walls, too, sketches and drawings and bits of calligraphy, some matted and some not. There was even a sort of clothesline hung with rectangles of paper clipped up by one corner, all showing the same angular portrait of an old man. Woodcut prints, hung up to dry, Barney Cotter had told her. He'd come into the house with her the afternoon the job began, when he'd had to chauffeur her over because she couldn't get her driver's license until next morning. It was Barney, too, who had identified the contraption with the steel roller and big spoked wheel as an etching press—he'd got very knowledgeable about art equipment when he had the maintenance job at Coast Community College. Hanna took his word for it; she wouldn't know an etching press from a sausage grinder. She did recognize the old proofing press taking up half the side wall. It looked a lot like the old Vandercook in Mr. Porch's print shop—the second foster home back before the Cotters. It was she who'd told Barney what that was.

Actually, Hanna mused as she walked toward the window, Barney was pretty decent, letting her borrow his jeep all the time so she could hang onto this job. It was the best job she'd ever found, the only real one. And whatever it took she was going to keep it and squirrel away every dime, before they could send her on to still another foster home. She *had* to get out of this rat race. On her own terms.

23

And soon. The thought of even one more foster home gave her a sort of scarey feeling—like something with a sputtering fuse. Barney seemed to grasp that, though they hadn't talked much about it, really. She wondered, sometimes, if he felt that way too, for reasons of his own.

Anyway. There wasn't any intruder in this house, so whoever had spilled those crumbs had dematerialized or something. Crawled back into the woodwork—maybe literally. It could have been mice.

Hanna made a mental note to ask Samantha—who had gone through the house the day the owners left—if there'd been any crumbs around then, and with a last glance toward the ocean, turned to leave the art room. Instantly she turned back, her retinas still registering a flash of red. Quickly she scanned the narrow wooden deck outside the window, the few fringes that were visible over the retaining wall of the tangle of salal and brush and horsetail that covered the rocky slope down to the beach. Nothing red there. Her imagination was working overtime, that was all. As Mrs. Porch always used to be saying. Or was it Mrs. Blackman or Mrs. Thomas or one of the others . . .

She climbed the stairs again, made another trip to the curbside mailbox and this time found the mail, came in sorting it roughly into catalogues, envelopes and junk, and stacked it on the coffee table with the growing accumulation. Then she finally fetched the watering pot and made the rounds of the plants, two clusters of pots in the living room and one in the big bedroom upstairs. And that was it, she thought regretfully as she tipped the last drop over the little jade plant in the bedroom window. Time to go back to Cotters' and do the breakfast dishes and collect Mrs. Cotter's cleaning and then take the jeep back to Barney.

Instead, she lingered, leaning on the wide sill and finally dropping luxuriously into the fat little comfortable chair beside it, letting her head fall back against the cushions and her eyes fill with the sparkling expanse of the Pacific. Samantha wouldn't like her sitting down. Well, Samantha wouldn't know. Samantha was too uptight anyway about what she called Proper Behavior in the Client's Home. She scarcely even wanted you to touch anything, just bring in the mail, water the plants, feed the damn goldfish and get out. Granted, they were Samantha's clients; it was Samantha's house-watch business and Samantha's responsibility if anything went wrong.

But I'm not hurting anything, Hanna thought, letting her mind relax into unaccustomed softness. I'll bet the owners wouldn't care a bit if I just sit here a minute and pretend it's mine.

And if they did—too bad.

The fact remained that she had to get the jeep back to Barney by noon. With a sigh she stood up—

and spotted that flash of red again, among the bushes clumped alongside the retaining wall. This time it did not vanish, or allow itself to be dismissed as imagination; in fact it remained perfectly still so that by moving a cautious step to the right and craning her neck a bit, she was able to identify it as a patch of red knit shirt on a crouching back. A small back —boy-sized. Somebody playing hide and seek? He was definitely hiding, whoever he was, between bushes and wall just to the right of the gap where a gate used to be and a long flight of wooden steps went down to the beach.

That might explain his earlier vanishing. If he'd been coming up those steps, then dived out of sight behind the bushes, he'd have gone right out of her sight as she stood at that basement-level window. Whereas from up here, he wasn't hidden at all . . . But had he ducked away because he'd seen her? Was he hiding from *her*, then? From whoever might be in the house?

Instantly she thought of the crumbs. Not mice, a boy—likely nosing around for something to swipe. But crackers seemed a funny choice, when there were umpteen other swipables lying around—a nice little radio, a mini-camera, that calculator she'd fiddled with herself the other day, a Swiss army knife lying right here on this windowsill—every one of them just right to slip in a pocket, all readily salable, as she was very much aware. And all still here. Besides, how could he have got in?—and out again, come to think of it, leaving everything locked and bolted behind him. Didn't make sense, it must have been mice after all.

But for an instant longer her thoughts clung to the puzzle, and her eyes to the patch of red—and so she saw it move, change to a mere pattern of color among the leaf-forms and emerge at the other side of a bush as the head and shoulders of a dark-haired boy, eleven or twelve years old, she judged. He was peering toward the house, anxiety in every cautious move, even consternation. Obviously, he'd spotted her in the art room window—or seen the jeep. That bit of the drive would be plainly visible from the steps. So why wasn't he heading out of here as fast as he could go, instead of trying to come back? If he was training as a sneak-thief, he was flunking.

For the first time, she wondered who he was. A neighbor kid? But these were mostly weekenders' houses, and the weekenders had gone back to Portland until next Friday. A runaway, maybe. It dawned on her that he could have been in the house all night—had the crackers for dinner, slept in a bed . . . The thought was scarcely completed before another burst upon her with jarring force.

The Polish kid. The one the hassle was about. It had been all over the papers for a week, even on the network news.

What was his name? Sounded like a place, or a cow, or . . . Jerzy, that was it. Jerzy Stepan Something-Unpronounceable-Beginning-with-W. He was

American-born, though. Only his folks were Poles. That was the crux of it, as she remembered. Because now his folks, who'd been living in Portland, wanted to go back to Poland, the idiots, and take him with them. Naturally, he'd refused to budge. She didn't blame him a bit.

There was a lot more to it that she couldn't remember. But one thing she knew: this morning's *Coaster Times* had said the kid had vanished into thin air yesterday—run away.

And Hanna Holderith had a good notion where he'd vanished to. She had a good notion she was looking at him right now. *He* was still looking fixedly at the jeep—waiting for it to go away, so he could get back into his hideout.

So now what do I do? Hanna asked herself, sinking down again into the little chair.

Nothing. Pretend you never saw him. Let him get away with it if he can, said an old Hanna, buried deep inside her, who was still ten years old.

And lose my job? demanded the other Hanna instantly. Fat chance! It's not my problem. Let Samantha sort it out.

She stood up, walked to the phone on the hall table, and dialed swiftly, listening to the crisp, efficient little clicks as the wheel spun back. Waiting for the ring, she carried the phone to the window seat, and resting one knee on the cushions peered out to locate the spot of red. It was closer—the boy had squirmed behind a big driftwood log that edged the bushes and lay stretched out, his eyes still riveted on the jeep. They were enormous eyes—dark and frightened and suspicious under straight black brows. Hanna stared at them as Samantha's number rang once, twice.

She hung up quickly, before the third ring. Nobody home, more than likely. No sense letting it ring forever, she could try again later.

And what if she didn't try again later? Half-kneeling there in the window seat, still staring at the boy and clutching the phone as if it might summon Samantha in spite of her if she didn't keep it gagged, she loosed her imagination cautiously, then boldly, letting the fantasies expand and rise like many-colored balloons until the air above her head was full of them, bumping softly together and tugging at their strings.

What if she plain and simply kept her mouth shut? Let the kid hide if he could, pull his whole scheme off—get free of the courts and the cops and all the grownups in the world and run his own life for a change? What if she even helped him? Brought food, and left it where he'd find it—not bothering him but just letting him know somebody was willing to go to bat for him, give him just *one* lousy person on his side. He might begin to look on her as his only friend, the only one with guts enough to stick up for him against everybody . . . Maybe in the end she'd go with him to the judge, make an impassioned defense . . .

Yeah, yeah, yeah. And her father was an Austrian count.

Look at that face. She knew very well what he was feeling, what he'd been learning the hard way these past days. She'd been learning it for sixteen years. At least she could talk to him, warn him that you couldn't trust *anybody*. Not the social worker, not the Sisters at the home, not the foster-parents— even the good ones—least of all your own parents who had simply swept you under the rug as a big mistake and got out fast. That is—his parents hadn't done that she supposed, but . . .

What if they did go back to Poland without him? He was awfully—small—to be on his own.

Oh, Lord, the courts would get him. The foster homes.

Well, *I* can't take care of him, Hanna thought in a sudden panic. I've got my own plans. It's not my problem. I'm no heroine. I'm not interested in medals.

The balloons were bursting all around her—*bang, bang, bang*—and she set down the phone, still watching the boy, but differently now.

So he better not trust me, either, she told herself with a shrug.

She wheeled away from the window, ran downstairs. She'd call Samantha from Cotters'. When she felt like it. *If* she felt like it. Meanwhile let Fate or something take charge. She wasn't even sure it *was* that Jerzy Whatsit. The kid might be anybody. Might not have the slightest intention of coming back in this house when she was gone. Might never have *been* in this house to begin with.

She paused at the living room archway, then detoured around the far side until she could stoop behind the goldfish tank for a peep out the windows. From this level she could just glimpse a scrap of red showing through a broken place in the driftwood log—she'd never have noticed it if she hadn't known where to look. He was a pretty good hider. Too bad he'd forgotten that second-story window.

As she watched, goldfish drifting occasionally across her line of vision, she felt a smile tugging at one corner of her mouth, felt a familiar slight malice stirring in her. So what if he was camping out in the house? It was kind of funny, really. This grand place with a view, the grand owners off somewhere on a grand vacation, paying Samantha for looking after their precious stuff . . . and Samantha with her prissy lectures about Respecting the Owners' Property, and never sitting in their damn precious chairs or touching the damn cameras and calculators and binoculars they left lying around like trash . . . and here was this kid camping out in the place, using their baby-blue plumbing and leaving cracker crumbs around.

Served them right. Served everybody right.

I'll clean up your crumbs for you next time,

31

Hanna told him silently. If there is a next time. If you're really the Polish kid hiding out there. If I don't tell Samantha about you first.

It occurred to her that there might be a way to find out whether or not this boy was Jerzy Stepan Whateveritwas.

She went out swiftly through the kitchen, setting the spring lock on the back door and testing it before she walked across the breezeway deck, down the few steps into the empty carport and through it to the jeep. Without a glance toward the beach, she backed into the driveway's elbow, drove forward into the street and headed back toward Tenth. Two houses farther along she turned sharply into another drive, cut the motor, and hurried back on foot. Dodging behind the spread-out limbs of the big spruce and keeping her head down, she followed the line of shrubs that masked the carport and ducked underneath the wooden slats of the breezeway. Stooping, she moved forward among the posts until the slope dropped away enough to let her stand upright, concealed by the stair climbing at right angles from the lower deck. Cautiously, she peered between the steps. And there he was—she had a head-on view of him from here—still flat down behind that driftwood log, still staring suspiciously at the place where the jeep had been.

Smart kid, she told him grimly. Never trust anybody. *Anybody.*

They waited, both of them, for a good five minutes. Then very carefully he moved, crept from his log to a tangle of summer's-end flowers at the edge of the grass strip, finally half stood up for a wary glance all around—preparatory, Hanna was certain, to a dash for the house.

Before he faced her way again she was gone, and two minutes later the jeep was rumbling on toward Tenth.

Plenty smart kid, Hanna was thinking with a curious exhilarated sense of satisfaction.

It wouldn't do him any good, of course. She'd have to blow the whistle on him. A dirty shame, but she wasn't going to risk her job for some kid, even this one. Not Hanna Holderith. She'd tell Samantha —if he was still there tomorrow.

THREE

It was okay, finally. That red-haired girl had gone.
He could go back in.

He hurried across the grass, feeling goosefleshy at
all his narrow escapes. It was pure chance he'd happened to come outdoors for a while—and just when
he did, neither earlier nor later. It was plain, pure
chance he'd spotted her at that playroom window
even before he saw the jeep. If he'd been looking
some other direction . . . it made him go cold all
over. He'd have walked right up these steps and in
the back door and probably come face to face with
her.

Now if he just hadn't goofed and left some traces
of himself around . . . he knew he'd put away the
blanket and pillow. Any water drops on the bathroom washbasin would have dried by now. He'd
hung up the towel.

Jerry let himself in the back door with the spare key he'd found hanging as always on the old key rack just inside the hall closet. Pausing only to reset the spring lock, he bounded up the stairs and into the guest bedroom—now the den. The corner cupboard was still closed. He yanked it open, saw his backpack still lying there on the floor with the straps in a kind of G-shape, exactly as he'd left it. With a long *whoooosh* of relief he backed up, dropped down limply onto the little couch.

Everything okay, out of sight, and even if she'd come into this room she apparently hadn't opened the closet. Hadn't spotted him out the playroom window, either, or she wouldn't have turned away so soon. And nobody could have seen him behind that log. But he'd better find some safer place to hide his backpack after this, if *she* was going to be tramping in and out. Of course, she probably wouldn't. He couldn't see any reason why she should come back.

But why was she here in the first place, that's what he wanted to know. Walking right into Gran's house just as if she had a right to—it burned Jerry up. What could she have been doing?

He got up, started on a tour of inspection to find out.

It took him a long, puzzled while to find a clue.

By that time he had noticed a lot of other things he wasn't looking for and would rather not have seen—and had failed to see some he would have given anything to find—such as Grandad's big old walrus tusk with the scratched-in pictures of walruses sitting around on ice floes. That tusk had always stood on the mantel above the fireplace, arching nearly halfway across it. Now there was a copper pitcher or jug or something there. Or Gran's sewing gadget that always stood beside her chair upstairs. He remembered it well—a wooden bowl on legs, always filled with a jumble of bright-colored spools of thread and scissors and stuff, and a little sunbonnet-girl cut out of faded purple felt, stuck full of needles. There was nothing beside the chair now, though the chair itself looked a little familiar. At least it was the right shape—kind of round and fat —though it was bright yellow and newish-looking, instead of faded blue with white flowers, so he wasn't sure it was the same.

A lot of the furniture looked a little familiar. But then all chairs and tables looked a lot alike. Downstairs in the west end of the living room there were two chairs, big leather ones, that looked entirely *un*familiar, and sounded so too. He'd sat down on one this morning and nearly jumped out of his skin at the sudden snort it gave as a lot of air or something all squashed out of it at once. When he'd poked and pushed at it experimentally he couldn't feel anything in the seat cushion *but* air, so maybe that was what they were stuffed with. It was a new one on him. And it really made funny noises as it let you slowly sink down. He had to admit those chairs were comfortable. But they weren't

Gran's and Grandad's when *he* used to come here.

In fact he had yet to spot one piece of furniture he really and truly recognized, remembered clearly from the old days. Such as the old blue velvet couch —twice as big as the one he'd slept on last night— the one he'd spilled the ink on, and Gran had said it didn't matter because that couch was older than Jerry's dad anyhow and overdue for a new cover. The dark green one in the living room now wasn't it. Not even a new cover could have made it look that different—it was a whole new couch.

So maybe they bought some new furniture, Jerry told himself, trying to shrug it off. People do that, dummy. And maybe they decided goldfish were a lot less trouble than dogs.

He supposed people even took up brand new unheard-of hobbies all of a sudden, too—if that's what all that stuff in the old playroom was about. Two great big machine things and pictures all over the room, and a squillion felt pens and pencils and stuff—but there used to be *games*, and the game table with the four white chairs, and a little record player, and a big box of toys Gran always dragged out when he came to visit, and crayons and coloring books. The way that room looked now really bugged him. What did they want all that art stuff for? Gran always said she couldn't draw a straight line, and Grandad . . . Jerry couldn't help smiling a little as he remembered Grandad's one and only picture, a kind of little cartoon cow he would solemnly draw every time you asked him to draw you a picture.

And when you asked him to tell you a story, Jerry reflected as he left the all-wrong playroom and climbed the stairs, he always said his rememberer was busted and he'd read you one instead. And he'd do it, too—he'd read as long as you'd listen, and do all the animal parts in squeaky high tones or scary roaring ones, until his voice got all clogged up and he'd wind up coughing and laughing, and Gran would tell him to stop before he choked.

Oh, I *wish* they were here already! Jerry thought with a wave of longing so fierce and sudden he had to stop in the front hall and hang onto the newel post.

He made himself let go of the post. They weren't here. But they'd *be* here. Right after Labor Day. That was the thing to hang onto—that one thought. He'd lived through one day already, or part of one. He could get through the other five or six. And if Auntie Marta's baby happened to have been born sooner than they expected, then they'd come home sooner.

Only don't count on that, he warned himself as he started upstairs. Don't count on a thing. Just find out about that girl.

He wondered if he really remembered Auntie Marta or whether the face in his mind was just one he'd made up, a kind of toothpaste commercial lady who looked like his dad. She was probably as neat-looking as he thought, because Dad was really handsome—everybody said so. And she was Dad's sister. She'd never seemed like an aunt, though, because he'd seen her so seldom. And her baby would probably never seem like a cousin, either.

He wished he could have at least one lousy *cousin*. He wished he had some kid really *related* to him— part of *his* family. Instead of...

He jerked himself loose from that thought. He was never going back, so none of that mattered. Find out about the girl.

Upstairs, he stopped in the middle of Gran's and Grandad's bedroom and looked all around, thinking irritably that it would help if he knew what he was looking for. The stupid girl wouldn't go dropping handkerchiefs around with her name and address on the corner, and even if she did—

A sudden sparkle caught his eye—something shiny in a little plant on the windowsill. He went closer. It was a drop of water, that was all, lying on one of the fat green leaves like a tiny crystal ball, and the sun made it glitter. The plant had just been watered.

The plant had just been watered.

Quickly Jerry checked the pots at the other end of the sill, and the fern on the bookshelf. They'd all been watered.

Immediately it began to make sense to him. You went away for two weeks or so, and you got somebody to come take care of your plants, and feed your goldfish, and all that. Probably she was a neighbor or something. No, because a neighbor wouldn't come in a jeep. Anyhow she must be somebody his grandparents knew. And she'd be back—maybe tomorrow. He wasn't sure how often goldfish had to eat. He'd better always be outdoors, and hidden, in the mornings, until he got her schedule straight. If she had a schedule. What if she just came any old time she thought of it?

Oh, well, thought Jerry, relaxing suddenly. It wouldn't matter that much if she did catch sight of him. He had a right to be here, this was his own Gran's house.

His thoughts paused, caught on the same nagging uneasiness that had plagued him since he first found the house last night. It *was* Gran and Grandad's house. How could it not be? He could even remember the wallpaper, knew where the key rack was, for cripes sake. So why couldn't he quit worrying about it?

Because I don't see Gran's and Grandad's stuff, came the whispered answer from inside him. I don't see the tusk. I don't see any pictures of *me*.

His breath sucked in sharply. *That* was something to look for. That would prove it.

There was a little picture frame on the dresser—he rushed to pick it up, studied the face of an old man. Not Grandad. Well, it could be Gran's long-dead brother or somebody. There were pictures in the hall . . . Not photographs, though, he found when he ran out to look at them. He was sure Gran used to have some pictures of him, he remembered her showing them to him—in a book. An album! That's what he must look for.

He found one—more than one, a whole row of them—in the bookshelves beside the fireplace in the living room. They were full of photographs; babies, children, teen-agers, grownups of every age right up to about a hundred, including several of the old man in the frame upstairs—every one of them strangers. He didn't recognize a single face. It was somebody's family—but not his.

This was somebody's house and furniture and stuff. But not Gran's and Grandad's.

But how could that *be*? His frantically roving gaze fell on the neat stacks of mail on the coffee table. He scrambled to his feet, leaving albums scattered on the rug, and snatched up a stack. Boxholder, Current Resident—he pawed until he found an envelope with a window. *Mr. E. G. McDowell.* Another—*Mr. and Mrs. Edgar McDowell.* A letter addressed in slanty handwriting: *Helen McDowell.* Magazines, all for McDowell. All at 1314 Sandpiper Road. Which this was. Not one thing addressed to Mr. or Mrs. Harold L. Starbeck, who were Gran and Grandad.

Finally, protestingly, still unbelievingly, he faced the answer he had been trying all along not to guess. It was the right house—but the wrong people. Mr. and Mrs. Edgar McDowell lived here now. Grandad and Gran had moved someplace else. They'd simply forgotten to mention it when he saw them last week.

They wouldn't, they *wouldn't* forget that! he kept telling himself, long after he'd begun answering wearily, Well, they did. Or maybe that baby at the restaurant drowned them out. Maybe they moved so long ago they took it for granted I knew it. Maybe they figured I wouldn't care. Why not? Why not *anything*? Look at all that's happened already.

So what now? It was all over. He'd have to go home. He dropped down onto the dark green couch that he had no right to sit on, leaped up as if it had burned him, and stared hopelessly around this almost-familiar room, once so beloved, where he had no right to be. Everything was wrecked. He couldn't stay here. Those McDowell people might come home any minute and find him. He might even be arrested or something—he'd broken in. He'd stolen their crackers and peanut butter, and this morning some Wheat Chex. He'd have to get out right away—and he had no place to go. No money, even, except about seventy-five cents, left from buying the bus ticket, which was a lot more expensive than he'd imagined. He'd have to hitchhike back to the city, and he'd never done that before and had been absolutely forbidden to, but he'd have to anyway. And then . . .

Then *what*? He began to walk around the room, unable to keep still, as one possibility after another revealed itself to be as much an impossibility as ever. He couldn't go home. Nobody there, and he didn't have his key any more, he'd turned it over to Whatshername, Vicky's Aunt Carol. And he couldn't go to Aunt Carol's house, he didn't even know where it was. And *besides.* What could he tell them? That he'd been with Dad all this time? So then they'd want to know why he wasn't still with Dad. Dad might even have got in touch with that Aunt Carol by now, finally remembered the arrangement . . . No. More likely not, Jerry thought bitterly. Anyway, probably even Dad didn't know where she lived.

To phone Dad himself was out of the question. He was never going to phone Dad again, never go anywhere with him, even a movie, never agree to another "arrangement." Dad was *finished.*

And he couldn't, *wouldn't,* phone his Mom at the Inn of Seven Sisters, no matter what she'd said. He couldn't imagine asking for "Mrs. Walter Fox" instead of Mrs. Hal Starbeck. Anyway, it was supposed to be her honeymoon, for cripes sake.

Not much of one, just a lousy week, fifty miles from home, but he supposed even a week without working, without cooking or errands or chauffeuring your kid, would seem pretty great. Especially since after this she'd have four kids to come home to instead of one.

No, Jerry told himself fiercely. There'll only be three. *Because I'm not going to be there.* She won't be lonesome. She'll have Vicky and Jeanne and Tom. And Walter Fox. I hope she's satisfied. I thought we were fine just the way we were, but no. Well, now she's got a crowd. She'll never even miss me.

So what else *was* there? Nothing. No place to go —except here. It was just like Sunday—yesterday— all over again, only worse, because yesterday he'd been sure Gran and Grandad would be home in a week. Could he call *them*? At Auntie Marta's? No, because he didn't know Auntie Marta's number or married name—or even what town she lived in. Just "California" was all he'd ever heard. And that was *it*. All the doors were closed. Even worse than Sunday.

He sat down heavily on the long window seat, recoiled as he remembered it wasn't Gran's and Grandad's, then defiantly went slack again. He was here, he was going to sit on it. He had to sit somewhere.

It *wasn't* worse than Sunday. Even with this last door closed. Nothing could be worse than Sunday. Maybe nothing would ever be that bad again. (There, that's one cheery note, he told himself sardonically.) At least now he was all by himself, without a lot of Foxes watching him, so if he wanted to look tensed up and miserable and humiliated and more and more desperate he could do it, and not have to keep a casual, no-expression expression on his face or try to act relaxed. If he wanted to bawl, he could bawl—he could yell and hit things and pound this window seat cushion—nobody would hear or care. He'd wanted to do all those things Sunday—all day Sunday—worst of all between one and two o'clock. But now that he could throw any kind of fit he liked, somehow he didn't care. It was just too late.

Sunday. Yesterday. Slumped on the window seat with his gaze on the hypnotic flutterings and driftings of the goldfish, he let his thoughts just barely touch Sunday, draw back fast, touch again—then before he could stop himself it was all happening again before his mind's eye like some awful, hateful movie.

First the wedding, with a lot too many dressed-up Foxes all over the place, and all their cousins and inlaws and old buddies, and practically nobody that belonged to him and Mom except her friend from work. And Mom in a new dress, looking excited and as though she wasn't really hearing him when he asked her something—and that dumb *tie* he had to wear and the place that kept itching where he couldn't reach all the time the minister was talking ... and then that "breakfast," they called it, though it was nearly lunchtime and at a big restaurant with waiters and all, and he had to sit with Vicky and Jeanne and Tom and pretend he thought it was okay they were going to be his stepsisters and stepbrother —and *they* were pretending too, he could tell—and it went on for hours and hours, and all the time he kept trying not to look at Mom way down there in the center of the long table beside Walter Fox, and trying not to think about her never being Mrs. Hal Starbeck any more, not ever again, and wondering what life was going to be like now.

And then . . .

Jerry yanked his eyes away from the goldfish, jumped up and began to walk rapidly around the room, trying to halt the hateful movie of Sunday. But it went right on like a dream you can't wake up from—he was already watching the taxi leave, the last flutter of his mom's hand in the back window, feeling the tug on his sleeve as Vicky kept yelling to come *on*, come *on*, Aunt Carol was ready to go— then in an unfamiliar back seat with Jeanne and Tom each staring out a side window and him staring straight forward at the back of this unknown Aunt Carol's shiny brown head and Vicky's mussed blonde one with the green plastic barette holding a wilting rose—and everybody silent, except for a few brightly stupid remarks from Aunt Carol which thunked like dead tennis balls.

Until Jeanne suddenly remembered about the swimming. "We get to go to that pool right down the block from Jerry's house. I mean *our* house."

Jerry sensed, rather than saw, her swift, uncertain glance at him. Obviously he wasn't the only one wondering what life was going to be like now.

"—and Jerry's mom said—I mean Enid said—"

Vicky took over, bossy as always. "*I'll* tell her,

Jeanne. Aunt Carol, Enid said it was a neighbor-
hood pool and always with a lifeguard and we could
go swimming awhile before we go to stay at your
apartment if it's okay with you, and I brought our
suits along in the suitcase, so is it okay?"

"Well, I—" A flash of blue eyes in the rear-view
mirror at Jerry, who pretended not to see. "I'm not
sure Jerry would have time for that before his dad
comes for him. When is he coming, Jerry?"

"About one. Or one-thirty," Jerry amended—just
in case. Carefully indifferent, he went on, "It's okay,
you can go on and swim. I'll just wait at the house
for him."

"Oh, we'll wait with you, won't we, kids?" Bright
smile in the mirror, another down at Vicky, beside
her. "*Then* we can swim for a little while. That be
all right, Jeannie-baby?"

Jeanne muttered a grudging assent, and the ten-
sion already building in Jerry tightened like a spring.
He said, "I don't *need* anybody to wait with me.
I've waited alone lots of times."

Unexpectedly, Tom said in his funny, gravelly little voice, "Yeah, Jerry's *twelve* already. Pop says we
won't even need to have a sitter now, 'cause Jerry
can be it."

Jerry barely had time to feel a surprised gratitude
for the support before he was wishing Tom at the
bottom of the ocean, gagged and handcuffed, because once started, he went right on.

"Jerry's gonna be my big brother, just like Billy

47

Moss's and we're gonna be roommates and he's gonna teach me stuff and show me how to shoot baskets and play checkers and—"

"Why, isn't that *lovely*, Tommy—"

"—and walk me to Cub Scouts and let me ride his bike sometimes, and—"

"Who says?" Jerry demanded, outraged.

"Pop. And you're gonna help me with my 'rithmetic, and—"

"*I* never said you could ride my bike. Besides, it—"

"And I can take the bus to the liberry if you're with me, and—"

On he went, like a nonstop rippling brook or something, until Vicky turned in her seat and yelled, *"Shut up!"*

Tom shut up, scowling. Vicky glared threateningly a moment, blue eyes wide, then flounced around to face front again. Aunt Carol said something peacemaking and dumb. Jeanne was obviously still brooding about the swimming pool. Jerry began to count the blocks still to go before they reached the house and he could escape from this car, this family of strangers he had got trapped into, this "den of Foxes," as his mother had called them once in fun.

It wasn't fun for him. Nor, he suspected, was it going to be fun for her, once the new wore off and she had to start coping with Walter Fox's kids. So far none of them—with the possible exception of

48

Tom, whose Pop must have given him a big pep talk last night—had shown any more enthusiasm for their rearranged life than he felt himself.

The car had barely stopped before he was out of it, climbing ruthlessly over Tom and striding across the grass to take the front steps in one bound. He had the key—for one last hour or so it was still *his* house. His and Mom's. Shoving the door past its usual stuck spot, he was first into the cool, familiar hall. He stood an instant, taking a last look at the key in his palm, then tossed it on the table for Aunt Carol to find, and strode on to his room, barely making it inside with the door shut before the others entered the house. Half expecting to hear Tom's feet hurrying along the passage after him, he turned the bolt. For one last hour he had no roommate. In fact, for one last week.

Swiftly he tweaked his backpack off the closet shelf, caught it, and began to pack, hoping against hope against bitter experience that Dad wouldn't be late *this* time. Surely he wouldn't. Not today.

Underwear. His running shorts and that real thin shirt in case it was hot up at Dad's. Long-sleeved red knit one in case it was chilly. Socks. Swim trunks— *he'd* be swimming in the lake, not just a stupid pool, and every day, too. What else? Toothbrush and stuff was in the bathroom. Get it later.

He yanked off the choking tie, the good shirt and pants, pulled on jeans and his navy T, stuffed a second pair of jeans into the pack, along with his harmonica with the chromatic key, a length of cord for practicing knots and the Drive-U-Crazy puzzle Dad had given him last birthday. It did sort of drive him crazy, but it would please Dad if he brought it. And that was enough stuff—more than he'd need. He'd probably spend most of next week in nothing but swim trunks, out in the boat with Dad, fishing. Or if they couldn't stay at the cabin all week, then riding around with Dad, and waiting in the car while he called on Good Prospects, and eating steak for dinner at restaurants and maybe going to a movie or a big basketball game before driving back to the little bachelor pad to sleep on the daybed. It was worth all the waiting in the car just to be with Dad the rest of the time. Jerry didn't mind that kind of waiting— it gave him time to practice using the chromatic key. He wouldn't mind *anything* if only Dad wouldn't be late today.

He peered out the window, craning to see the driveway between the big rhododendron and the corner of the house. No big gray car yet, only Aunt Carol's little orange one. But then it wasn't quite time. Anyway, he was ready. He picked up the backpack, stood a moment at the door glancing around the room that was all his for the last time, then turned back the bolt and went to collect his toothbrush and comb. By the time he slouched into the living room full of Foxes it was exactly one o'clock.

They'd changed into their bathing suits—all except Aunt Carol. Jeanne and Tom were kneeling on the couch by the front window, watching the drive-way. Vicky sprawled in the big chair with her legs draped over the arm, her nose in a library book. Aunt Carol was in the other chair turning the pages of Mom's *Sunset* magazine.

"You might as well go on swimming," Jerry said casually. "He'll be here in a minute."

"Oh, no hurry at all, is there, kids?" Aunt Carol looked up, beaming. "All ready, are you? Got your toothbrush?"

"Yeah," said Jerry. He shot a look out the window, lowered himself temporarily onto the little straight chair nearest the door.

"Well, I know you're going to have a *grand* time. I wish *I* were going to the lake!"

Jerry said nothing. He looked out the window again, *willing* the gray car to turn in the drive, the familiar white smile to flash under the dark moustache. Aunt Carol returned to her magazine.

Ten minutes later she put it aside, as Jeanne said for the fourth time, "Why doesn't he *get* here?"

"He's a little late sometimes," Jerry said hurriedly. "He must've got hung up. Why don't you guys go on to the pool?"

"Now don't you worry about us and that pool. We've got till three o'clock before we have to start for my place. Jeannie-baby, you and Tom quit *watching*. That'll bring him quicker than anything. Say!" Aunt Carol sat up straight, glancing around with wide eyes. "Anybody want to play a game?"

Jeanne and Tom were half interested. "What kinda game?"

"Well, let's see what we can *find*! I'll bet Jerry's got some games around here . . ."

Before Jerry could find a way to stop it, Tom had remembered the dominos, and the three of them were settling down around the dining table. Vicky kept on reading, after one expressionless glance at his face. He got up, walked to the front door and looked out the screen for a while, wandered back to his chair.

One domino game had ended and another begun when Vicky glanced up again. "Maybe he forgot," she said.

"Forgot!" cried Jerry. He gave a crack of laughter that sounded twice as loud as he'd intended. "He wouldn't *forget*, are you nutty or something? He's hung up, that's all."

Vicky looked at her watch, then shrugged and returned to her book.

"I just hope he hasn't had an accident," Jerry added sternly.

Again the noncommittal blue gaze fixed on his face. "You think he might?"

"No! For cripe's sake. He's a great driver. The best. He'll get here. Probably got the time mixed up. He does that."

No comment.

The domino game finished in a burst of "No *fair!*"

52

punctuated by laughing exclamations from Aunt Carol, and pretty soon started all over again. Jerry went outside and sauntered to the corner to look desperately down empty Thornton Street, and sauntered back again barely able to drag along the great lump of lead inside him. By then Vicky had finished her book and moved over to the couch to stare out of the window. Jerry dropped onto the arm of the chair she'd left, his back turned to all of them, both hands clenched fiercely on the straps of his backpack.

Dad wasn't coming. He knew it. It was one of those times. He was never this late except when he'd forgotten all about it. It had "slipped his mind"—or "gone right out of his head," as he always said afterwards, with that shamefaced laugh, always ruefully admitting it was all his fault, always feeling so bad, and eager to make it up to you. And he did make it up to you. Next time you and he did something so really great that it just wiped the other hurt away, dimmed the memory, so you always forgave him. Dad was easy, easy to forgive. Even those times when it hadn't slipped his mind but he just didn't show up. Like when it was the circus, but Dad suddenly had to fly to Lake Tahoe with a client, only you didn't know it, and went on waiting at a certain bus stop for hours and hours until people must've thought you lived there. And like the three separate times you were all packed to visit Gran and Grandad but every single time something came up, and Dad couldn't get away—or even to a phone, so once you'd missed a Scout cookout too, just waiting. But that time he'd been stuck in a business meeting—naturally he couldn't go hunting for a phone in the middle of an important meeting. And once he'd had to take a Good Prospect to dinner. And anyway, how could anybody phone somebody at a bus stop?

Dad had always been easy to make excuses for.

But not this time.

Not today.

Not with Vicky already guessing the truth, with everybody hanging around bored to death and wanting to go swimming and blaming him and thinking bad things about Dad and wishing they could get *rid* of him, and probably beginning to wonder if they weren't going to be rid of him for the whole *week* . . .

Jerry's skin was beginning to prickle all over as if he were wearing a wool shirt, and his cheeks felt hot and queer and his breath wouldn't settle down. He'd never felt so in the way—never wished so hard to vanish through the floor. He *couldn't* go to Aunt Carol's apartment, there was no room. She'd said herself there was just the daybed for Vicky and Jeanne and a sleeping bag for Tom. And they couldn't stay here because Aunt Carol had cats and her little shop to look after. *He* was the only headache. He had to get out, take himself off somehow, remove the big, lumpish, boring, insoluble problem he'd turned into.

"Well, my *goodness*, Jerry!" exclaimed Aunt Carol, and he spun around to see her looking at her watch. The domino game had finally broken up. "Two o'clock! Do you suppose—"

"He's got the time mixed up." Jerry was on his feet, talking rapidly. "Probably thought Mom said two, not one. I think she only talked to his secretary. Listen, you guys go on to the pool—you're using all your time up. He's bound to show up in a couple minutes now."

"But I don't quite like to . . . what if something's happened to prevent him, and he—"

"Well, then I'll still be here when you get back, won't I?" Jerry shrugged and spread his lips in what he hoped was a careless grin, though it felt more like baring his teeth to the dentist, and his dry upper lip hung up on his eyetooth and had to be grimaced free.

"Why, yes—that's so, of course!" Aunt Carol put a forefinger to her cheek a moment, then turned gaily to the others. "Okay, you swimmers, let's go! Say goodbye to Jerry—and if his dad hasn't come when we get back, why, we'll just say hello again!"

And so finally they went—in a glad rush, throwing back a few "bye's" without looking, Aunt Carol picking up the door key and waving it at him with a last bright smile. A minute later the little orange car backed out of the drive and sped away down the block.

Jerry gulped down a sob that hurt his throat as if he'd swallowed something wrong-end-to. Now to go. Get out of here. Somewhere, anywhere. He didn't *know* where.

And then he did know.

He hesitated just long enough to rob his cigar box in the dining room buffet, saying a grim goodbye to the new camera he was saving for, only hoping there was enough for the bus as he stuffed the few bills into his wallet and the change into his jeans. Then, snatching his backpack, he opened the front door, cautiously peered after the orange car. It was just disappearing around the corner of Fortieth. Quickly he set the night lock, made sure the latch caught. Then he set off at a run in the opposite direction.

And now here he was, slumped on the long window seat staring at the goldfish weaving their watery paths, listening to the burbling of the little pump and the vast mutter of the ocean in the silence of an empty house where he had no right to be. And all the problems were still unsolved, all the impossibilities still right there, just like Sunday—yesterday. He could not go to Aunt Carol's. He could not go home or to a motel. He could not mess up the honeymoon of that sudden stranger, Mrs. Walter Fox—or let *Mr.* Walter Fox know what his own father had done to him. And he could not, would not ever again make any arrangement of any kind with Mr. Hal Starbeck, formerly known as Dad.

Jerry found himself on his feet, just standing there, not even seeing the room but seeing plainly what he must do. It was the only thing he could do—stay right here.

And suddenly he felt calm—or, not calm exactly but lumpish, inert, like a big chunk of something that has come immovably to rest. It was a relief not to feel much of anything. This was going to take some working out, and he'd have to make some plans.

That girl—how to avoid, he thought, outlining it like a school composition in his head. *Food—how to find enough. Clues about self—how to conceal at all times. Jeep—how to keep watch for.*

His feet took him toward the kitchen. He was hungry right now. Starving. There was food here— in the kitchen, in the dog room. Gran and Grandad would have been glad for him to take anything he could find. But these McDowells wouldn't. What about that? Nothing about that, he decided with his new lumpish indifference. He'd just take it anyway. Steal it. He'd have to become a thief.

He moved impassively here and there, opening cupboards, the refrigerator, the freezer, scanning the pantry shelves. He could survive for quite a while—there was cereal and peanut butter, canned soup and sardines and jelly, crackers, some canned beans and things, a frozen loaf of bread and a little frozen butter, even a part-carton of ice cream.

He transferred most of the ice cream into a bowl,

digging it out with the only ice cream scoop he could find, which looked like a genuine antique. Then he took it back to the living room and made plans while he ate. He'd have to keep close watch on the street and driveway. The instant he spotted that jeep he'd run down to the playroom and out that door, escape down the beach steps and hide on the slope, or go on down to the beach. He'd have to keep his dishes washed, his blanket put away, his backpack . . . What about the backpack? She might look in the closet next time. Keep it with him, then. At all times. Then when he had to run, he'd take it along.

Okay. All settled. He could feed himself, he could stay hidden, it would work.

It would work until those McDowells got home from wherever they were. He had no idea when that would be.

Now take it easy, Jerry told himself, hanging on hard to his stony calm. When you see the Mc-Dowells coming just follow the rules, grab the back-pack and get going, and that time just—keep going. And stay gone.

Stay gone *where*? And for how long—forever? He'd only looked as far ahead as next week, when Gran and Grandad would be home and everything would be different. But they'd never be coming home to *this* house.

Jerry leaped up and took his bowl and spoon to the kitchen and washed them, ordering himself furiously to cool it, cool it. He'd figured out enough for one day. There was no sense getting in another panic.

Carefully he dried the spoon and bowl, put them away and hung up the dishtowel. Then he went upstairs into the little den and turned on the TV.

FOUR

Hanna climbed out of the jeep Tuesday morning whistling and cheerful. She had worked it all out overnight.

This afternoon, when she phoned Samantha to make her regular every-other-day report, she'd say, "Oh, by the way. You know the morning after the McDowells left, when you went in to make the list of things I was supposed to do? Well, did you notice any crumbs scattered around in the kitchen?" and Samantha would say no, she certainly hadn't, and then Hanna would say she *thought* not, and then she'd report that she'd seen some today (not yesterday when she'd really seen them) and caught a glimpse of a boy coming up the steps from the beach, who'd run away when she called to him— and she'd thought of that newspaper story and did Samantha think it might be the Polish kid, hiding in the house, and should they phone the police?

But before she phoned Samantha—*well* before—she was going to locate that boy and warn him she intended to blow the whistle. She'd hunted up the details of his story in the paper last night. Jerzy Stepan Wrenskjold, his name was—however you said that. He was an Oregon-born, full American citizen, and had civil and constitutional rights and the whole bag. The catch was, he was a minor. And his folks, who were his legal guardians, were full Polish citizens and wanted to go home to their troubled country, for reasons far too Polish and emotional for a mere American to comprehend. And they wanted to take Jerzy with them. Deadlock. Press and legal profession having a field day. Kid caught in the middle, about to be torn in two. The parents' plane was due to leave tomorrow. Day before yesterday the kid had vanished.

Hanna was on his side all the way. In fact, she intended to hunt him up right now, first thing, so he'd have plenty of chance to clear out and find some other place to hide before she had her little talk with Samantha.

She felt well satisfied with this solution. It gave this Jerzy Whatshisname a break without holding the slightest risk for Hanna Holderith, even winning her a lot of Brownie points with Samantha for being so alert and reliable and everything. And she could always use points. She frequently got the impression that Samantha didn't entirely trust her.

61

Quite a coincidence, Hanna thought flippantly. Since frequently I don't entirely trust myself. Possibly because I'm not entirely trustworthy.

That made her think of Barney and their running argument. She half smiled as she paused in the kitchen—it was slick as a whistle today, not a crumb in sight—to unsling her shoulder bag and toss it on the counter. Its strap broke as she did so, and she muttered, "Damn-damn-damn" automatically, examining the weak spot to see if it was still repairable. Maybe one more time, she decided. Talk about untrustworthy. Cheap purses were the most, the worst. Not that she'd ever had any other kind. Or known any other kind of people, whatever Barney said.

It was funny about Barney, she reflected as she filled the watering pot. He was stuck with cheap clothes too, belts that curled, and shoes that busted, and seams that were always pulling away from their stitches over his big shoulders. And he'd had almost as much experience as she with sleazy half-truths, and promises that lasted about as long as that purse strap, which was until they had to take a little strain. And still he persisted in this notion that you should believe in people. You should give them a chance. If they acted like marked-down sale goods when it came to the crunch, well, all right, that was their problem. But someday—

"*Their* problem?" she'd echoed indignantly last night, when they'd been rehashing it for the umpteenth time. "Listen, Buster, it's *my* problem when that fink Diane hides her boyfriend's grass in our locker, and then swears it's mine! Who d'you think got off free in that little fracas?"

"Well, that's what I *mean*, Red. That teacher should've trusted what you told her. She should've given you a chance!"

"She hasn't got your faith in human nature."

"And it put her in the wrong! She was wrong about you! Don't you see what I mean?"

Hanna had looked at him a minute across the half-cleared dinner table—the earnest, honest brown eyes, the truck-driver body and the teddybear inside —and sighed, but smiled because what else could you do? "Sure, I see what you mean. What *I* mean is she *wasn't* wrong about me. I knew that stuff was there. It wasn't mine, but I knew it was there. I'd told Diane to get it out or else, because I knew good and well what would happen, but she hadn't done it yet, that's all."

"So how come you didn't lower the boom?" Barney jabbed a triumphant finger at her.

"Because I hate to stir things up—they usually get dumped on me."

"No, Red. It was because *she's* the fink—not you." Barney gathered up a cluster of mismatched water glasses in one pawlike hand. "Y'see? You just proved what I said in the first place. That teacher had you wrong."

"Barney, for the love of . . . Sometimes I think

63

your head is made of solid Jello." Hanna was laughing as she carried a stack of plates to the crowded little kitchen. You had to laugh at Barney or you might cry or scream or something. She'd often wondered how he had got through life this far without getting a *little* hardened up or else bent all out of shape just for lack of self-protection. All those summers shucking shrimp and crab in the shop—all those Saturdays out in his cousin's boat in every kind of weather, helping to catch them—and all for free, of course, for the family business. When he'd finally got old enough for minimum wage they'd tossed him out and taken on the cousin's younger kid instead. Which left Barney hunting out odd jobs and night-watchman jobs to get through high school, and odd jobs and night-watchman jobs to creep his way through Coast Community College at the rate of about six credits a year. So here he was, at twenty-two, still living at home, up to his elbows in his mom's foster kids, helping with the dishes, and only getting a belly laugh when he talked about becoming a doctor.

A doctor! He had as much chance of being a doctor as Hanna had of being Queen of Sheba. And still he had this attitude that nobody'd ripped him off especially, that people weren't all jerks or finks, and that Hanna should find this out. He was frowning at her right now, solemnly, thoughtfully, as he eased the water glasses into the dishpan and turned on the water.

"It's Eddie's and Sharon's night to wash," she reminded him.

"I know—just getting 'em started. Listen, Red. You oughtn't to be so down on everything. Honest. Someday—I know I've said this a lot—but someday you're gonna find somebody you can trust. And then everything's gonna seem different."

"I'll hold that thought, Doc. Meanwhile you better get a move on, you've only got ten minutes before you've got to start watching the night."

Of course, Hanna reflected now as she fed the McDowells' goldfish, what Barney was trying to tell her was that *he* was somebody she could trust. Barney liked her more than a little bit, she sometimes suspected. Why, she couldn't imagine. Must have a taste for plain, pale, (sturdy) girls with red curly hair, she thought. Well, she liked old Barney too— who could help it? And she was sure she *could* trust him. Until the crunch came and he found it was going to cost him too much one way or another— some of his precious chemistry credits or something. Then he'd have second thoughts, or dodge the issue, or simply choose what was most important to him . . . like anybody else. She wouldn't blame him. By and large Barney was a pretty good sort. If she were going to trust anybody, he'd probably be first choice.

But all Hanna Holderith was going to trust was experience, and hers said, *Don't cash checks for anybody, ever*, in big red letters.

She poked an experimental finger into the earth

65

of the nearest plant, found it still moist, and went outside to get the mail. Very little today—one magazine, one bill, and two blahs. She started sorting them onto the coffee table, then stopped. The stacks looked different. They were neat and squared off—a little *too* neat and squared off, as if they'd been messed up first—and the junk mail was *left* of the magazines, the letters to the right, instead of the other way around as she'd left it. Hanna smiled. So he'd got curious, had he? Got to wondering whose house he was camping in. Well, she'd tell him all about it in a minute. She finished with the mail, went back to rebolt the front door, then unplugged the automatic turn-on gadget from the little lamp near the front window and moved it to the one between the two leather chairs. Have to keep those burglars guessing. Upstairs, she transferred the gadget from the little bathroom to a radio in the McDowells' bedroom, and set it to come on strong at noon and cut off at 12:45. Anything else? No.

Now to find that boy.

She had been glancing out windows whenever she was near one, but now she knelt on the bedroom window seat and slowly scanned the retaining wall, the bushes, and as much as she could see of the steep slope down to the sand. No flash of red—no sign of anything. That didn't mean he wasn't there somewhere, but she'd check the inside first, and this time *really* check it out.

She walked into the middle of the upstairs hall and cupped her hands around her mouth. "Hey, Jerzy!" she called. "The game's over. You can come out now!"

She waited. No answer, not a sound. She hadn't expected one.

"Okay, here I come!" she warned. Then she started.

Fifteen minutes later she stood at the art room window, slightly breathless and more than slightly exasperated, though she was beginning to be amused as well. Nothing. Not one clue anywhere. You had to hand it to that kid. He really knew how to cover his tracks—really wipe himself right off the map, till you were ready to believe you'd never seen him in the first place. Well, then, outdoors.

She left the art room door open behind her, walked to the end of the deck and paused to call again, twice—but softly. If there were neighbors in earshot she didn't want them getting curious. No response. She went on down the four steps and doubled back on the strip of grass to the break in the seaward wall where there had once been a gate. There were more steps here, the long rickety wooden flight with one handrail that led steeply down to the beach if you didn't mind risking your neck. Hanna glanced from a splintered and sagging step to one with a whole board missing, noted several toothless spots in the descending flight, and decided that beach-walking must be very low in the McDowells' priorities. Oh, well. This would be nothing to a kid.

Cautiously she started down, stopping often to study the tangle of brush on either side. A little past halfway she got clear of a big bulge in the slope's profile and found herself with an unobstructed view of the beach in both directions. It was a beach with limits. About a quarter-mile to the south a huge headland thrust out into the ocean, falling sheer to the water and effectively blocking the passage of anything without fins. Two stoop-shouldered figures, well bundled up, were trudging antlike toward it. To the north, a lesser barrier was formed by a creek emerging from its gully to spread out across the sands, shallow but much too wide to cross dry-shod. Even beyond the creek there was little to see: a couple of preschoolers and their sand buckets with a bigger girl and a deliriously barking dog chasing sea gulls; farther in the distance a lone man sitting on a driftwood log. Nothing else but birds and sea for half a mile, when another headland closed the view. No Polish boy, dry-shod or unshod, anywhere in sight.

Hanna turned back, no longer amused, aware of an odd sinking sensation she had no wish to define. She thought suddenly of one more possibility. Stumbling carelessly now up the dilapidated steps, she ran back along the lower deck, through the art room and into the little hall, where she flung open the door to the cubbyhole under the stairs. Black as pitch in there. She fumbled for the light, switched it on to reveal a row of old paint cans, the leaves to a table, plastic jugs of something, a worn-down broom. No boy.

There wasn't any place else to look.

"Jerzy! *Jerzy!*" she yelled, almost screamed, as if furious insistence alone could make him appear from somewhere. But nothing was going to make him appear. She'd scared him off after all—just that glimpse he'd had of her was enough. He was gone.

After a while she came out of the cubbyhole, turned off the light. The playroom door gaped open. She went across and slammed it with all her strength.

Slowly, heavily, she climbed the basement stairs, paused in the front hall to let the ache in her legs subside. She didn't know why she'd run so fast. She didn't know why she felt as if she weighed three hundred pounds and had no muscles. She didn't know why she should have this feeling of let-down, of bitter disappointment—almost of deep loss. She hadn't lost a thing. It was silly to get all worked up about it. Silly to care. That Polish kid was nothing to her, she'd intended to send him away herself this morning, hadn't she? It was just that it was unexpected, not finding even a trace of him.

She walked on to the living room windows and leaned there, staring at the sweep of ocean and wondering where he had gone. Where could he go? The paper this morning had merely said he was missing. Search still continuing. Fear of possible abduction, accident, et cetera, but the hospitals hadn't seen him and the cops had picked up nobody of his description.

He was just—gone. As though he had never existed, as though she had made it all up.

Exactly like that little kid at Murchisons'. Jimmy.

Jimmy. She hadn't thought of him in months—maybe years—but suddenly she was almost hearing him laugh, watching the grin crinkle up that homely little face of his until it was all teeth and freckles. He and she used to say they were really and truly brother and sister, not just foster, because they were both freckly. *And* plain, thought Hanna. *And* lonesome. But Jimmy's hair was far from red; it was black and straight as a Comanche's. For all she knew he was a Comanche—he could certainly let out a convincing war whoop when he was sick and tired of those leg braces and wanted them off for a while. She had often wondered if he ever got really well. They had said he might—the doctors at the clinic. But maybe they were just saying it. One thing she knew—he got to have a little fun for at least eleven months of his life, which was more than he'd had before he turned up at Murchisons'. To look at him that day—that rainy day he'd arrived—you'd have thought he'd never once smiled in his entire four years. Skinny, pale, solemn, with desolate dark eyes and that air of remoteness, as if nothing that happened had anything to do with him. He'd been in a hospital where a lot of the kids could run and play, at least a little. Not Jimmy. He'd grasped already that he was a sideliner for life, and he'd accepted it.

Hanna never knew why that got under her skin, or why—a scrawny, ten-year-old nobody herself—she was seized by a rage to make him fight it, make him laugh once, make him ask a question or learn to whistle or even yell bloody murder—anything but just sit and take it. She never knew why it was that from the minute he came to that house he seemed to belong to her, and she to him. She never felt anything but casual affection for the half-dozen other toddlers and first-graders—including Mrs. Murchison's own two—she helped with and hand-fed and mopped up after and hoisted onto potty-chairs in the three years she spent at Murchisons'. But Jimmy was hers, and she made him know it. She also made him smile, the second week he was there. A few days later he looked surprised—then curious —and a week after that he laughed. From there on it was all downhill, and everybody began to find out how his face crinkled up when he giggled and all about that Comanche yell.

She got him talking, too. At first he wasn't very good at it because he'd never bothered before, just sat and listened. But he learned fast, and once he did, he talked fast. First thing she knew she had a chatterbox on her hands and was wondering if she should ever have turned him on. He could ask forty

71

questions a minute. She answered—or made up answers—while she cleared the dishes or gave him his bath or held him up by the armpits while he took his labored five steps away from his chair and five steps back. And they made long-term plans. They were going to stay together always. When Hanna got to be sixteen and all grown up she was going to get a job as somebody's cook or housekeeper and he would be there too and she'd get a bike and ride him back and forth to school, and they'd be each other's family. That's what they'd planned.

And then one day she came home from school to find him gone. Just gone. Somebody had adopted him or something. They'd come from the agency. She never knew where he went, and never saw him again.

Funny, she thought mirthlessly as she walked into the McDowells' kitchen to get her busted purse. She didn't even know whether he'd lived or died.

Died, most likely. And here she was sixteen and all grown up with nothing but a little part-time job you couldn't support a flea on, so it was a good thing he hadn't depended on *her*.

Anyway this vanishing act today wasn't like that one—not anything like it. This Polish kid wasn't Jimmy. He was just somebody she didn't know. So snap out of it, she told herself. Keep your eye on the ball—your job, saving up the money, getting free.

In fact, what about calling the newspapers to let

them know he *had* been here? It might make him easier to trace—might keep something worse from happening to him. There might even be a reward for information . . . ? No, fat chance. Actually there was no sense in doing anything, he was gone and that was that. Those idiot parents of his were due to take off for Poland tomorrow evening. So either they'd go without him, or they'd stay and hunt for him, and whatever they did it was no skin off the nose of Hanna Holderith. It was nothing to do with her at all. It never had been.

Feeling a little colder, a little more drawn-up inside, than usual, she locked the door behind her and climbed into Barney's jeep.

FIVE

From his perch well up in the big Climbing Tree, Jerry watched the girl emerge from the kitchen door, cross the little covered deck, and disappear into the carport. She was moving as if she'd walked ten miles—not at all in the brisk way she'd been striding around the place for the past forty-five minutes. He had been catching glimpses of her all that time—first from the big maple down near the retaining wall, on the high platform that was the only bit left of the tree house he and Grandad had built one summer. You could see the ocean from there, and quite a bit of beach, and also right into the living room and the big bedroom upstairs, so he could see her moving here and there; she was easy to spot because of her hair. When she'd disappeared for so long that he'd decided to come down, all at once there she was walking out the playroom door, call-

74

ing something that sounded enough like "Jerry" to scare him to death for a minute. But she called again and it turned out to be "jersey." Weird. Then she went over to the beach steps and after a little hesitation, started down them. Jerry didn't blame her for the hesitation. Those steps were something. Grandad would never have let them get like that.

Of course he had frozen in mid-motion, the way wild animals had to do when danger threatened, and she hadn't spotted him or even glanced his way, though she was looking every other direction. That, and the calling, made it seem as if she was really hunting somebody, maybe as if she'd tumbled to the fact that somebody had been in the house and was trying to locate whoever it was. Why she thought yelling "jersey" would do it, he couldn't fathom, but at least it was clear she knew nothing about *him*.

As soon as she was well out of sight down the steps he came down from the platform in a rush, and ran around to shinny up the Climbing Tree so he could watch when she left. Then he was sorry he'd moved, because it seemed hours before she showed up again. He knew she was back from the beach, though, because he could hear her feet running on the deck, and a minute later faintly heard her yell "jersey" again, in a sort of muffled voice, as if she were hollering down a well. And a few minutes after that he heard the playroom door slam, hard. Then nothing. Boredom, and his foot going to sleep so he had to shift around and brace with the other one, and after a while shift back. Then at last, out she came dragging her purse by a broken strap and looking as if somebody had poisoned her dog. He wondered what had happened to put her in such a bad mood just in the last quarter-hour—because a glance at his watch proved he hadn't been sitting here for the hours it felt like. Maybe she'd turned on the TV and heard some bad news or something. Maybe she was just a weirdo, going around all over the place yelling "jersey."

She slammed the jeep door hard too. And gunned the motor the way you weren't supposed to do if you were a good driver—Dad said—and backed up with a jerk before turning to chug on out the short drive-way. The back wheel bumped off the curb as she made the turn into Sandpiper Road. She was driving as if she just didn't care. Jerry was just as glad he wasn't riding anywhere with her. She probably *was* a weirdo.

He wondered how she had found out somebody had been in the house. He'd thought himself per-fectly safe and unsuspected providing he kept out of her way. Of course, he probably *was* safe now. Safer than before. She must have convinced herself there was nobody anywhere around. Right now she was probably thinking she'd imagined it in the first place. Or just deciding whoever it was had gone.

She was gone too by this time—the jeep's special bass-voiced growl had died clear away. Easing his foot out of the pinching tree crotch, Jerry wiggled it to get the pins and needles out, then started down the tree, glad enough to go in the house and sit in a chair for a while. Trees were great hiding places, though. Once long ago, his dad had told him that people seldom looked *up*, and that somewhere above people's heads was the best place to keep out of sight. He'd always remembered that. It had really worked for him today, too.

His backpack caught on the snag of a broken branch and he tugged it loose impatiently. It was an awful drag, that pack—a constant *thing* he couldn't escape or get rid of. But rule number one for safe hiding was: never leave the pack behind. Already he longed to dump this nuisance in the ocean. How was he going to feel about it this time next week?

Suddenly, as he unlocked the back door and went into the kitchen, he knew he wouldn't—couldn't— be here this time next week. Those McDowells were bound to come home sometime or other. What's more, his mom would come home—not just "some-time or other" but next Sunday afternoon—and when she found out he wasn't at Dad's and wasn't at Aunt Carol's she'd lose her mind. You couldn't do that to your own mom.

Jerry sank onto the living room couch, letting the pack slide to the floor at his feet and giving it a kick. If I could get a message to her, he thought.

But what would the message say? Not: *I am at Gran's and Grandad's, don't worry.* Because as it turned out, he wasn't. How about *I am okay and not kidnapped or anything, don't worry?* Oh, fine. Great. He could just see her reaction to that one. Better to stick to the first message, even if it was a lie, only of course she would phone Dad right away and find out Gran and Grandad had moved, then she'd find out where they'd moved to . . .

For the first time it occurred to Jerry that *he* might be able to find out where they'd moved to. Only—how? For him, calling Dad was *out*. Would they possibly be in the phone book, here in Horseshoe Beach? They would if they'd only changed houses, not towns . . . and if they hadn't moved too recently to be in the book . . .

He was in the hall before he finished the thought, snatching the phone book from its shelf in the little table, fumbling through the R's, the S's—Stanton, Staples, Stapp . . . Stark. No Starbeck. Right on to Starkweather and Starling. He let the book flop shut, shoved it back in its cubbyhole. For a few minutes he just stood there in the hall chewing his lip and staring at nothing, while thoughts ran here and there in his brain like hamsters in a cage. About as useful, too. How did you find people when they'd moved?

He didn't know. He wondered what his long-term plan had been when he ran to get on that bus. Answer: he hadn't had one. Just to get to Gran and Grandad had seemed enough. He'd figured they'd take it from there. Well, now he had to take it from there himself; he had to think of *something*. He couldn't stay here beyond this week . . . What would

Gran and Grandad have done if they had been here? Phoned Dad? No, because he'd have begged them not to. Phoned Mom on Sunday, then. But *he* couldn't do that—not now. He'd have to tell where he'd been, that he'd broken into a stranger's house, stayed when he knew he had no right, stolen people's food and used their blanket . . .

He broke off his thoughts with an effort. It was only *Tuesday*. He had some more days to think. Maybe he'd wake up tomorrow morning with some great idea. Meanwhile it was time to steal some more of the McDowells' peanut butter.

He was just putting the lid on a sandwich when without the slightest warning, a blast of sound nearly jerked the hair right out of his scalp. Loud, frantic sound, and *close*—maybe upstairs, but *in this house*. He was out the back door, across the breezeway deck and down into the carport with a bound that ignored the steps, dodging around the posts and in another instant scrambling up into the Climbing Tree. Almost before he knew he had moved, he was in his old perch, with his foot in the same too-narrow crotch, his breath coming in uneven gulps, the sandwich squeezed almost in two in his hand . . . and his backpack, he belatedly realized, still on the kitchen floor in plain, tattletail sight.

He groaned, started hastily down to fetch it, shrank back sure he would arrive in the kitchen just in time to confront whoever was . . . Whoever was what? Whoever was upstairs.

But how could anybody be upstairs?

Well, somebody had turned that radio on—loud. *Deafening*. He could hear it from clear out here, bellowing something about soap flakes, with rock music and another yakkity-yak voice mixed in. Why didn't they turn it *down*? Or anyway unscramble the stations? You'd think anybody would . . . would . . .

Anybody *would* twist the knob, tune something in. Jerry's brain, abruptly beginning to function again, presented him with a clear picture of a green clocklike thing he'd come across yesterday morning that looked like an oversized kitchen timer, but on investigation had proved to be the gadget that turned on the living room lamp every night at dusk. There was another that worked the guest bathroom light.

That nutty girl had switched one of them to the radio, and reset the clock.

Irritably he unwedged his foot from the crotch, got down from the tree, and—not without a good many pauses and some very deep breaths—forced himself to go upstairs, enter the noisy, empty bedroom, and turn the radio down. Without turning it off, he tuned it to a single station. Then finally he went downstairs and ate his lunch.

The day was overcast, and the TV weatherman that morning had said it might rain later. Staring out at a vast gray ocean after he'd cleaned up the kitchen, Jerry decided to go down to the beach right away, while he had the chance. It would be awful, he thought as he ran down the back steps to the lower deck, to be cooped up all day in that empty house—time passed slowly enough as it was.

Whistling—and reminding himself immediately of the girl, who had been whistling nearly every time he'd seen her—he trotted expertly down the beach steps, avoiding the broken places and taking care his pack didn't catch on the splintery rail. But he stopped short as the view opened before him. *Everybody* had decided to take a walk now instead of later. There were people all over the place down there—he counted fifteen, plus two dogs, on this side of the creek, and he could see a few beyond. A lot of them were little kids, too, who would notice him—and notice he didn't belong around here.

Well, that was that, at least for now. Reluctantly he returned to the house, dumped the pack and looked around for something to do. Goldfish. *They* were no company. He wished the McDowells had a cat. Well, there was always the harmonica, and those new knots to learn. And after that he could see if there was anything on the TV, or maybe find a book to read.

It was after five when he woke up, dazed and stiff-necked, in the shadowy little upstairs den. The TV was still muttering and squeaking as cartoon animals scampered around the screen; the McDowells' book about treasure-hunting, which was what had put him to sleep, was still open on his lap. Outside the sun was shining—he could see that through the slits in the Venetian blinds. And maybe everybody was gone by now from the beach.

In five minutes he was far enough down the rickety steps to see that his wish was granted. The ocean, still mostly gray but with blue and green patches in it because the sun was shining through breaks in the overcast, was lapping at an almost deserted shore. There was a threesome of women beyond the creek, walking even farther away, a man in the other direction heading for one of the paths up to the street, and the inevitable dog in the distance —a big, bouncy, black one. Otherwise the gulls and the sandpipers and Jerry had it all to themselves.

Feeling a lot like the dog and almost wishing he could bark with the simple joy of freedom, Jerry ran and bounced and leaped and galloped to get the kinks out of his legs. Then, breathless, he trotted alongside the white-ruffled edge of the sea, dodging away now and then as a wave tumbled closer and closer and became smaller and faster and foamier until finally it hissed to its limit right at his heels and sank out of sight, leaving its scallopy outline in gleaming sand that swiftly dulled and winked and darkened to a firm, smoothed surface. There were other such outlines, traced in old foam and little broken shells and threadlike seaweed, overlapping each other in the dry sand just beyond the wet, where waves had reached and vanished before. Jerry judged the tide was coming in now, because each wave he dodged seemed to reach in farther than the last one. But he was usually wrong about tides. If Grandad were here, he'd know.

The sandpipers weren't bothering to dodge the waves; they ate something out of them. A dozen or so were skimming along ahead of him at the surf's edge, looking as usual as if they moved on wheels instead of feet. The low sun threw their long, speeding shadows across the wet sand, and turned the legs into thin bent sticks when they stopped to peck at whatever it was they found in the inch of water swooshing around their ankles. And the air was full of gulls. The high, rough rocks of the headland were full of them too—you could see their droppings everywhere up there, like spatters of white paint. They had their nests there, Grandad said. But they were still swooping and banking and hang-gliding, sometimes dropping down to ride in a dignified way upon the waves. Gulls had more fun than anybody, except dogs.

Feeling a little dizzy from watching them, Jerry turned his attention downwards. He found a pretty good sand dollar with only one jagged hole in it where a gull had pecked through to get a meal, and dozens of dark gray cone-shaped shells the size of a fingernail. A little farther along were a lot of the tiny colorless jellyfish that were everywhere today, left stranded by an earlier tide. They looked like funny little blobs of no-flavor gelatin except for the bluish fan-thing Grandad said they used like a sail to carry them along in the sea. By-the-Wind Sailors, they were called. Jerry tried to pick one up, but it only got sandy and lost all its strange, clear, blobby charm, so he started on toward the tidepools at the base of the headland.

It was then he noticed how much the shadows had thickened, there below the headland. Glancing seaward, he saw that the break in the overcast had narrowed to a long, low slit of pale green with gray veils drifting over it. The sun was a big red balloon in the middle, dropping visibly, inch by inch, into the dark cloudbank below. He slowed, turned to sight down the distance he had come, then reluctantly started back. He was a long, long way from the house.

He slung his backpack on properly so he could walk faster. You never realized how far you'd come until you started home with the wind in your face. There was always a steady, chilled breeze from the northwest this time of evening that got to your ears the minute you headed this way. The going was harder, too, now, mostly in loose sand—the smooth hard-packed strip was all but gone. He'd been right about the tide.

It was going to get dark early tonight. The sun had turned into a crimson smear across the west, and below, it was hard to tell where purple-gray clouds left off and purple-gray sea began. When he looked back again toward the tidepools in the shelter of the high rock they looked dim and cold, and some of the houses to the landward side showed

84

lights. He quickened his pace a little more, cupping both hands over his ears, but you couldn't walk that way, it threw your stride off. Better let the ears freeze and concentrate on hurrying. Once more he wished for his jacket.

By the time he reached the big driftwood log that marked two-thirds of the distance back, the crimson in the sky had faded to a murky streak, and it was beginning to spit a little rain. Great, he thought. Just what I need, to get soaking wet and leave tracks all over the house, and how will I get my clothes dry? He pulled the pack around far enough to dig his hand in and find an undershirt. With some difficulty —by now he was jogging, or slogging was more like it—he managed to tie it under his chin like an old lady's scarf. The relief to his ears was immediate, and there was nobody to see him anyhow. Nobody else dumb enough to be out this late, in this lousy weather, he thought. They're all in their nice warm houses, eating dinner.

The thought of dinner—even a can of creamed corn, even another peanut-butter sandwich—drove him along faster. Running in sand was like running in a dream—you worked and worked and scarcely got anywhere. But by the time his side was beginning to ache really unbearably, he was only a few yards away from the bottom of the rickety stair. Panting, he staggered through the last of the sliding, uneven sand and gratefully began to stumble up the steps.

He was not quite halfway up when one of them gave way.

There was a tilt, a jolt, a splintering noise, and nothing under him. His hands hit a step above with a stinging slap. His foot skidded sideways, twisted, then went straight through the space where the step ought to be and struck the tumbled rock beneath the stair. Something wrenched it violently into an impossible position and held it fast. His attempt to free it sent a shaft of pain up through his leg and a flood of panic through him. He struggled harder, cried aloud with the pain, and felt the world go black and nauseating for an instant.

Cool it, cool it, he told himself desperately. Rest a minute. Then try again—easy this time. Easy, easy . . . *Ohhhhh but I can't, I can't* . . . The dim, wet, rock-and-weedy world lurched around him, stretched and narrowed and twisted and squashed like an image in one of those mirrors in amusement parks, then grudgingly settled down into what seemed a very temporary stability. This time he stayed very still, so as not to stir it up again. His hands, outstretched on the higher step, were getting wetter and wetter. The rain was settling down too, and there was an awful feeling of permanence about *that*.

He took a long, cautious breath of the chilly air, felt a little less woozy, and made himself take stock of his position. He was lying flat out, with his head uphill, his hands on the second step above the broken one, his cheek, still swathed in the undershirt, on the first above, and the edge of the first one below the gap cutting into his left knee. His right leg stretched down and awkwardly sideways through the space, with the ankle twisted all wrong and the shoe wedged somehow in the rocks. He lifted his cheek, tried to see down through the broken place to what was holding his foot, but it was useless. Too much stuff in the way, even if it hadn't been lots too dim under there. And wet. And cold.

I can't *stay* here, thought Jerry. I'll get pneumonia or something. I'll die.

Frantically he jerked at his foot again, rode out the wave of nauseating pain again, breathed deep until the world held still. He couldn't yank loose, he couldn't see what was trapping him. He'd have to get the rest of him down there somehow, under the steps, close enough to *feel* what it was. Maybe . . . maybe get the shoe off.

He began some cautious squirming and immediately found the backpack hindering him. Wrestling it around to where he could slip out of the straps, he suddenly remembered the flashlight and felt a flutter of relief that he was at least beginning to use his head. In another minute he had the little golden circle shining down through the gap. A little further squirming and he managed to get into a position where he could see his foot.

It was wedged between a big, tough, twisted root and the big, immovable, half-buried rock the root had curled around—and the open part of the wedge was sideways, not up. His yanking had probably tightened the trap. Or else—he peered closer, stared in disbelief—the foot itself had tightened it. What he could see of his ankle below the hiked-up jeans had swelled already to mammoth proportions—probably his foot had too. It looked revolting—gross. And terrifying. He had a brief, vivid vision of a bleached skeleton lying right here on these broken steps, with its bony foot still caught in that trap. It gave him the will and the strength and the contortionist's ability to wriggle right off the steps and tumble through the gap, onto the weeds and rocks a couple of feet below. There he lay a moment, gasping, his face clenched like a fist as he endured the spasm of pain from his ankle. The rest of him was now scraped and bruised here and there as well.

But he could reach his shoelace now. As soon as he could breathe and open his eyes, he began to work on it. After an endless, weary, impossibly difficult time he got the laces opened enough, and the thick root bent aside barely enough, to worry his foot out of the shoe. It was unrecognizable when he dragged the constricting sock off. It was a horrible big fat shapeless balloon, and it was perfectly useless. But it was free.

He lay for quite a long while, too near his limits of fortitude to have much interest in what came next. But finally his own shivering roused him. He forced his sluggish thoughts to take some shape, to focus around some plan. His ankle was obviously sprained—it looked just like Elton Brook's had, that time at Scout camp. He was cold and clammy-damp, and sooner or later he'd be soaked through, because the rain obviously wasn't going to stop. And the dark had come. It seemed almost too much to imagine, getting back up onto the stair, somehow dragging himself to the top. However, he made a stab at imagining it, and then a stab at doing it. No use. It was too much.

End of the line. End of his great vanishing act and his great, muddled plan which had just ended in a big mess anyhow. Nothing left to do but yell for help.

He turned his face upward to the gap between the steps and tried to yell. It came out a sort of breathy mew—like a kitten noise. He took a breath and tried again. This time it was more like a gull noise. He gulped air, gathered all the strength he had into his chest and lungs, and made a desperate try for volume. This time you could call it a yell. He was absolutely sure it could be heard within a radius of ten feet from where he lay—and probably not an inch farther. There was too much background noise —the rain, the gusty wind, the incoming tide. And he was down in a kind of hollow, just to make it worse. It wasn't going to be any use to yell. Nobody could hear him.

If somebody would *come*, he thought. Anybody.

89

Even a dog, to bark at me and make a racket so people would know I'm here. If I only had some way to signal, or . . .

The flashlight. Maybe somebody would be on the beach, hurrying home—or on the path up to the street, or . . . Already he was flashing the little light, holding it at arm's length straight up through the gap in the stair, flashing it in a desperate SOS, three shorts, three longs, three shorts—pause—three shorts, three longs, three shorts. He kept it up until his arm gave out and he had to rest, then for another while until he realized the batteries were giving out too.

It was no use anyway. He visualized the dark, empty beach, the deserted path, the vast, black ocean, with his one little spark of a light flickering its SOS to nobody—and the vision was so dismal he hurriedly blocked it out. Better to forget all that lonesomeness out there and try to do something about right here under the steps, while he had any juice left in those batteries.

The feeble circle danced from lumpy rock to scrubby, stunted bushes that were little more than a tough bare stem tipped with a few ragged leaves. The embankment was not an encouraging place for things to grow. But a couple of yards uphill, on the other side of the stair, a clump of salal had found nourishment enough to spread and thicken, forming a low umbrella over a patch of ground. His light barely reached it; but if *he* could, he might find that

90

patch was dry. Without giving himself a chance to think about it, he switched off the light, hooked one arm in the pack straps and began to inch his way under the stair.

It was far worse than running through the sand, than trying to climb somewhere in a dream, because he had to drag his swollen, pain-filled foot behind him over rocks and sticks and twisty roots and all the other obstacles he could neither see nor avoid. Time stretched like elastic, leaving him panting just where he'd been an hour ago—or maybe five minutes ago. He had to push the undershirt-scarf back off his head; his neck was sweaty with exertion, and his face burning up, though the rest of him was freezing. But he reached the clump of salal at last, thrust an arm deep under the low, scratchy shelter of twigs and leaves, and the ground was dry.

He knew what he was going to do now, and while he had enough strength he did it. Clinging to the slope on one elbow, he took every item of clothing out of his pack and began to put it all on. Two more undershirts, the real thin shirt he'd brought in case it was hot at Dad's—if only this *were* Dad's, if only it *were* sunshiny hot—and the red knit long-sleeved shirt over the blue T he was already wearing. Then his extra jeans—though the right leg wouldn't go on over the swollen, excruciating iceberg that was his foot. The underpants and swim suit he stuffed back in the pack to pad the hard edges of puzzle and harmonica and wallet, and make a pillow. The socks

91

he pulled over his frigid hands. Then he eased the horrible bare foot into one leg of his running shorts, just enough to give it some kind of cover. Holding the shorts in place with one fuzzy paw, he wormed his way under his skimpy shelter, curled until there were no parts of him sticking out into the wet, and after a final struggle got the undershirt-scarf back over his head and the pack jammed more or less adequately under it. Then he drew a long, explosive breath and let every muscle go limp.

He was safe—for a while. At least he wouldn't get pneumonia—he didn't think. He wouldn't starve until tomorrow, though he felt as if he were doing it right now. He was a little warmer already and not getting any wetter. The thing to do now was sleep.

He was so tired he did sleep, until some dark, lost, no-time hour in the night when he was wakened by his foot and ankle throbbing like live things, with a fierce, gigantic pain. And the foot felt *hot*, though the rest of him was cramped with cold. He groaned and tried to touch it, felt a twig jab perilously near his eye and gave up the attempt, trying instead to squirm into a different position, get the foot higher somehow. It was on the downhill side, and you were supposed to elevate a sprain—he remembered that from Elton's. Supposed to or not, he couldn't do it. Nothing worked. He tried to ignore the whole thing and go back to sleep. That didn't work either, for a long, long time, when finally he fell into a weary doze.

From there on, the night became a nightmare—of waking and dozing, shivering and throbbing pain, trying to find a better position, a little comfort, a little warmth. He thought of his jacket, at home hanging uselessly in his closet, with a longing that was almost frenzy, visualizing in yearning detail its fleecy lining, its snug collar, until the image stayed with him through his brief naps and even figured in his dreams. By the time he opened his eyes at last to find he was beginning to see the wet rocks and weeds, that the dim gray of morning was spreading, he knew that any effort, any pain, was better than staying another hour where he was.

He was stiff and cramped and clumsy with layers of clothing, some of it only half on. But he was afraid to leave it behind; it was his only protection. At least the rain had stopped, though not the chill, steady wind. And soon he'd be able to see where he was going.

Where *was* he going? As the gray lightened into the prosaic, dull daylight of an overcast morning, he weighed the uninviting possibilities. Downhill was the broken step, the scene of his disaster. The stair ran close to the ground there, where a rock outcrop humped up beneath the long slant of the supports. He might get up onto the stair again through the broken place. But he'd have to go back *downhill* to get to it. He couldn't bear the thought of giving up the ten or twelve feet he'd won so laboriously last night. Uphill, then. Just crawl on the ground, and forget about the stair? It might be easier or harder; he couldn't tell. And he couldn't see to the top, from his worm's position.

Start anyhow, he told himself. Just *go*. On your way.

He edged out from under the bush, using mostly his elbows, until he was clear enough of branches to get his good foot up under him and give a cautious but strong shove which sent him several inches up the rocky, uneven face of the slope. So all right—he had started.

Of course, the pain had started again too, with renewed enthusiasm. He gritted his teeth and kept going, clutching at weeds and bracing his hipbone against half-buried rocks. Occasionally something gave, and he slid back a precious few inches while dislodged pebbles rattled down past him, bouncing off his tender foot. Above and around him the gray air was filled with the cries of gulls far and near, and the vast, resonant sound of the ocean, like a thousand voices gossiping—as if the world were one huge conch shell held to the ear. Close at hand perception narrowed to magnified details of flattened wet weeds and crumbling stones, the reek of salt and wet earth, the noise of his own arduous puffing. After ten minutes during which he gained another six or eight feet he was forced to stop and wait for the pain in his foot and ankle to subside to reasonable proportions.

Waiting, he tried out an idea he would have dis-

94

carded as absurdly impractical at any other time: he managed to work the nearly empty backpack, which he was still dragging stubbornly after him, under the injured foot, then he wound the straps around one wrist. When he started hitching on again, he kept an even pull on the straps, and tugged pack and foot along together like a little sled bearing a wounded passenger. It worked much better than he had hoped. At least the torn and muddy running shorts which served as blanket quit catching on every rock and root, and there was more padding under the foot as it bumped helplessly along, sending arrows of pain clear up into his thigh with every hitch.

By the time he was forced to rest again he had covered half the distance before him, and was past the bulge in the hillside that had kept him from seeing to the top. He could see the whole way very well now, and the next bit was a little less steep. Unfortunately the bit after that—the last crucial stretch up to the top and over—was quite impossible. The retaining wall, barely hip-high on the side next the house, showed its full four-foot height on this side, with an almost vertical two-foot drop just below it. The stair slanted down across the drop-off like a bridge—a bridge too high to clamber up onto without a good strong jump. Good strong jumps were out of the question—almost unimaginable. But a few yards down from the top, almost directly across from where he was now, the stair came close to the ground.

Laboriously, he dragged himself and his mud-caked little sled across to the spot, pulled himself up by a post to examine the stair—and found that the worst of the old gaps were all *above* that place. Underneath the gaps, the ground fell away too sharply to risk a fall.

Jerry lowered himself back to the ground, put his cheek down on some coarse, wet grass and gave up, just for a minute. Just for the luxury of ceasing to struggle, of not even planning to struggle. But after a while he hoisted himself onto one elbow and peered wearily around. From here he could see right under the stair, and up to the top on the other side. And there on the far side of the stair, close under the wall, was a place that was not so steep. If he could get there, the wall would be only shoulder-high, and there was a place to stand, below.

He stared at it awhile, then grasped the straps of his wounded passenger's transportation and began hitching uphill again to a spot where he could angle under the stair. There was only one thing to do—get to the wall and wait for that girl. She'd show up eventually, in about two hours. The way he felt right now it would take him that long to get to the wall.

He made it in twenty minutes, found a patch of weeds at the base of the wall to stretch out on, against a twisty bush that would keep him from tumbling clean down to the bottom if he relaxed. He had done all he could do for the moment. Exhausted, considerably warmed by his exertions, and inured

by now to the constant throbbing of his leg, he slept
—and almost missed the jeep when it came.

It was a crow that woke him, jeering stridently at
the world as it flapped away just overhead. Jerry
scrambled back to consciousness and then, heedless
of pain, out of the weeds to the wall, pulling himself
upright somehow, anyhow, to stand on his one leg
with both arms flung across the top. The jeep was
there. A glance at his watch told him it might have
been there ten or fifteen minutes—she'd be all finished and leaving soon. He'd meant to catch her
when she came, yell at her when she was still outdoors and as close as the carport. He yelled anyway,
as loud as he could: "Girl! *Girl!*" But he only
sounded like another of the wheeling gulls—he
could hear it himself, a thin, piping cry thrown away
against the world-filling background noise of the
ocean. He needed a crow's lungs, an elephant's
lungs to carry over that. If she would look out a
window—but she wouldn't be hunting for anybody
today, she thought he was gone. He'd taken care to
convince her he was gone. His gaze clung to one
window after another anyway, moving desperately
from dining room to living room to playroom; the
upper windows were too high, they were only a
streak of mirror from here. And in one of his
glances toward the playroom he caught a glimpse
of her—pale face, bright hair.

"*Girl!* GIRL!" he cried—another gull mewing—
willing her to come back to the window and look

out. As if his eyes had stared a hole in the glass to attract her, she did come back. She stood and looked at the ocean, at the treetops swaying—everywhere but at him, though he was waving one red-clad arm frantically, and his leg was so bad, hanging down unsupported and throbbing, that he knew he couldn't wave much longer.

She started to turn away. And saw him.

She froze. Then she vanished from the window as if something had yanked her backwards. An instant later the playroom door burst open and she was running across the grass.

SIX

If it hadn't been for those heart-stopping eyes and his dead-white, rigid face, Hanna might have burst out laughing when she got a closer look at him. That absurd, muddy little clown hanging there on the wall like a discarded doll, with his head swathed as if for toothache, wearing his socks on his hands and what looked like the rest of his wardrobe bunched up around arms and shoulders.

She reached him, at once alarmed, swept with unreasonable joy that he was still here after all, bewildered. "What *is* it? What . . ."

"My foot," he whispered.

She peered over the wall, and lost all desire to laugh. "Hang on, I'm coming around."

She moved as fast as extreme caution would permit; what neither of them needed right now was for her to join the ranks of the casualties. In a moment or two she was beside him on the seaward side of the wall, looking for level ground to plant her feet.

"Okay, Jerzy, listen. I've got to stand right where you're standing, it's the best spot. So kind of lift your feet and hang by your arms just a second, while I crowd in there behind you. Then I'll boost you up onto the wall. All you gotta do is sit there, while I come back around. Okay?"

"Okay," came the thread of an answer.

Hanna carried out this operation as outlined, scrambled thankfully off the treacherous stair and safe onto the grass, and hurried back to where she'd put him. He was sagging as if the doll had no stuffing, as if only the layers of clothing held him up. She caught his drifting gaze and held it. "I've got to get you to a doctor."

The eyes focused quickly. "No."

She wasn't at all surprised. "I'm not sure you can do without one."

"Please . . . I'm so cold. Hungry."

"You're also hurt."

"Not much. Sprained ankle. You just prop your foot up high. Please. Not *yet*."

She studied him, thinking fast. He looked all in, shivering with cold. She daren't call in the Cotters' doctor anyway. She'd have to hunt through the phone book for one who didn't know her, get the address. "Okay, not quite yet. But sooner or later, so get that straight. I don't want you coming all apart for lack of medical attention and have it my

100

fault." She added fiercely, "And believe me, if you fold up before I can get you off my hands, I never heard of you, see? I'll just toss you back over the wall."

He met her stare, and after a moment the wraith of a smile tilted the corner of his mouth. "Okay."

Kid's got a sense of humor as well as guts, she thought. She reached out to untie his head-swathing. "Halloween's a month or so off yet," she told him. "What were you going as, Marley's Ghost? . . . Good lord, it's an undershirt."

"Please, can we go inside now?" He was unfocused again, and sagging.

"Can and will, but it's not my house, Jerzy. I've got to get the muddiest stuff off first, or we'll both be in trouble. Just the top layer, okay?"

"Yeah."

She worked fast but gently, peeling off the mudcaked sock-mittens, the red shirt, the extra jeans dangling from his one good leg. She dropped the lot on the grass beside a couple of unrecognizable mud pies that had fallen off by themselves when she set him on the wall. Then she scooped him up and headed for the lower deck, feeling like an ant carrying an especially long-legged spider. Thank the Lord for "sturdy" along with "plain," she thought as she maneuvered his terrible-looking bare foot through the door and across the art room. And thank the lord he was only long, instead of heavy. The awkwardness, and the care it took not to bump that swollen ankle were enough to cope with. By the time she got him to the foot of the stairs she was puffing, but she started up anyway, counting on momentum and will to see her through. Halfway up she had to stop to let her legs quit wobbling.

"Just a whistle-stop. Won't be a minute," she panted.

"Sorry. I'm awful big for you."

"Nah. Got Amazon blood in me. Here we go."

She made it to the top this time, and staggered down the front hall into the dining L, where she eased him into the biggest of the chairs—the one with arms. Thanking her stars they were covered in vinyl, not velvet, she pulled another one nearer and got his feet up, raiding the kitchen drawers to assemble a thick, soft pad of dish towels to raise the injured one even higher.

"Only temporary, but I've got to get some of that mud off before I dare put you on the couch." She was stripping off her windbreaker as she spoke, wrapping it around his shoulders. The top half of him was dirt-smeared but had been partially protected from the wet by the layers of clothes she'd discarded outdoors. The right leg of his jeans, unprotected by anything, was a sodden, gritty mess, and looked too narrow to get off over his swollen foot and ankle. She stared at it, daunted. "Too bad you don't go in for wide-leg pants. I may have to cut these right off you. How long you been *out* there, anyhow?"

"All night."

She looked at him quickly, while words like *exposure, shock, hypothermia* flashed across her brain, half-forgotten signals from a mostly-forgotten eighth-grade health class. She remembered enough to head for the kitchen. "Well, say goodbye to the pants. First priority is to get you warm, even if I have to take you to the doc in the altogether . . . Maybe I can get your other pair dry somehow . . . do the best we can."

Still talking, she pawed through a drawer for the kitchen shears, turned on a burner of the slow-heating electric stove on her way back to him.

"Hold still now." Firmly, swiftly, she cut away the sodden jeans, leaving him his underpants, taking off the filthy left sock and shoe. "Where's the other one?"

He blinked at her wearily, hugged the windbreaker closer. "Down on the hill somewhere. Under the place where the step broke. It got stuck and I had to leave it—I couldn't get loose."

"You don't say?" she murmured. "How come you didn't just gnaw your paw off?" She had the jeans spread back so he was free of them. "Here we go, only one more journey and I'll quit bugging you. Hang onto that windbreaker, just keep it around you."

She deposited him on the living room couch, eased one of the fat throw pillows under his swollen leg and spread the afghan over him. Then she raced upstairs, collected more pillows and a couple of old green-checked comforters from the linen closet, and raced back to bundle him up like a mummy. He was shivering convulsively and clenching his jaw. Weighing the advantages of warmth inside against warmth outside, she took another five minutes to find and fill a hot water bottle and tuck it under the covers with him.

"Now. Warm up, get me? I'm going to fix you some soup."

The burner was glowing red by now; she got a can opened and its contents heating before she fetched in the hall phone on its long cord and began searching the yellow pages under "physicians."

There were only two in Horseshoe Beach proper; they both knew her. In Fisherman's Bay, ten miles down the coast, there were a dozen strangers listed; it was a much bigger town. She chose one at random and dialed.

"Dr. Phillips's office."

"Uh—I'd like to bring somebody over, if I could, in about—"

"Dr. Phillips isn't in the office on Wednesdays."

"Oh. Thank you."

And get lost, thought Hanna. She dialed another number.

"Fisherman's Bay Clinic. Which doctor did you want, please?"

"It doesn't matter. Whichever one is—"

"You're not a regular patient here?"

"No, but—"

"The doctors are attending the AMA meetings in Portland this week. Unless you're a regular patient—"

"Look—it's sort of *urgent*. It isn't for me, it's a kid with a sprained ankle, and it's all swollen, and—"

"I suggest you take him to the Emergency Room at the hospital in Seaside. They'll be able to help him." Click.

I'm sure they will, Hanna thought savagely as she banged down the phone. And they'll have to help me too, once I've carried him twenty miles on my back.

Emergency Room . . . she was suddenly remembering all the questions they asked you at hospitals, even at doctors' offices, before they let you much past the door. Name, address, phone, ID. Name of parent or guardian if a minor. Do you have insurance? If not, what arrangement . . .

Good lord, what am I doing? she thought. Who's going to pay for all this? Who's going to fill out all those forms and cut all that red tape and . . . She backed away from the phone, then stopped. Barney? *He* wasn't a minor. What's more, at a little past noon—about an hour from now—he'd be driving to Seaside anyway for his one o'clock class . . .

Risky. She'd have to trust him with the whole story. With Jerzy. No. Not even Barney.

Then how about if she just phoned and asked him

what the hell to *do*? He'd know. He'd probably taken a seminar in sprained ankles. She could say she was having this argument with a friend—made a bet . . . Her hand hovered a moment over the phone, reluctantly drew back. Barney was no dummy. Better not.

Who, then?

The druggist! She reached for the phone, mentally kicking herself for not thinking of it before. Old Man Nicolson—he loved to hear your symptoms, he prescribed as solemnly and readily as if his name was Mayo, and he wouldn't ask about—

"Corner Pharmacy, Nicolson speaking."

"Oh, hello Mr. Nicolson." She spoke quietly, hand cupping the mouthpiece, turning as far away from the living room as the cord would reach. "Why —uh—this is Mrs. O'Pfluhnflm, and my little girl seems to have injured her ankle, and I wondered—"

In five minutes she had it—elastic bandage, under the instep and around up the leg and back down under again, prop it up good, cold packs for thirty-six to forty-eight hours, then hot wet soaks. "You'll find it responds pretty fast, Mrs. Errr. Of course, if you think it might be broken—"

"Broken! Well, I—how would I be able to tell?"

"X-ray's the only way. If there's still a lot of pain after a week or so, better check with the doc. But he wouldn't be able to cast it till the swelling's down anyway."

"I see. Yes. Thank you very much."

Hanna hung up, stared uneasily into midair. Broken? With any luck, not. Over to me, she thought. All of a sudden I'm head nurse as well as rescue squad. One thing's dead certain—I can't pay for any X-ray.

The soup was boiling over. She snatched it off the burner, poured some in a bowl, found a spoon, carried it into the living room. He had quit shivering, and was lying with his eyes closed in his green cocoon, looking very small and weary, but he opened his eyes as she approached. They were dark and enormous in his white wedge of a face.

"Oh boy, does that ever smell good," he whispered.

"Have at it, then. Wait, I'll put a pillow behind you." As he began eagerly on his soup, she added, "Your foot still hurting?"

"Yeah."

"Probably because I've got it too nice and cozy. That deep-freeze treatment it got last night was the best thing for it, I just found out." She was uncovering the foot and ankle as she spoke, then tucking the covers back tightly from the knee up.

"*How'd* you just find out?" The spoon was poised halfway to his mouth.

"I made a phone call. Looks like you win, Jerzy. No doctor. I give you first aid right here, today, and tomorrow we see how it is. Okay?"

"Yeah," he breathed. His face relaxed, his eyes were suddenly darker and more liquid than ever.

"Thanks a lot. Thanks for *everything*. I'll be lots better tomorrow."

"And anyhow, that plane'll be gone by then," Hanna said drily.

"Plane?" He actually looked blank.

"Don't give me that. Now get the rest of that soup inside, while I raid the medicine cabinets. You're supposed to have an elastic bandage, though I don't suppose I'll find one."

She headed for the stairs, leaving him staring at her. Let him work it out for himself. The sooner they leveled with each other, the better, in her opinion.

She failed to find an elastic bandage, but she found the McDowells' ragbag, with most of somebody's old knit undershirt among the scraps of towel and sheeting. There were scissors in the little bathroom, even a safety pin; she took everything downstairs and after a little fumbling, and some advice from the boy himself, achieved a reasonably efficient-looking job with strips of undershirt. While he finished his soup she filled an icebag she'd turned up in the medicine cabinet, and bound it firmly in place on his bandaged ankle. Then she picked up his empty bowl.

"Want some more?"

"Oh—I dunno. I wish there was some milk."

"I'll get you some water." She brought him a glass, along with the rest of the soup. "Just in case," she said, putting the bowl on the coffee table within

108

easy reach. "You're looking less like Marley's Ghost already, you know that? I'm going outdoors now, but I'll be back."

In the dining room she collected the ruined jeans and his left shoe and sock, plus the smudged dishtowel off the top of the stack that had propped his foot. But on her way through the little utility room beyond the kitchen she stopped short, eyeing the washing machine and dryer lined up beside the freezer. She'd had the laundromat in mind, but this would be quicker. And safer. And cheaper.

Just make yourself at home, dear, she thought as she dumped her gritty load in the washer. Samantha will be so pleased.

Letting herself out the back door, she went down again to the grass strip behind the house. One of the mud pies, she saw now, was a small school backpack with some lumpy things inside it. She fished out a puzzle, seventy-seven cents, a length of cord, a harmonica, and a very flat wallet. She stuffed these into her jeans and shirt pockets, and after knocking some of the half-dried mud off against the retaining wall, added the pack to the pile of his other belongings. Then she went to peer doubtfully down the treacherous stair. The wind had half-dried it too; in fact, the sun was feebly trying to shine.

Come on, all you can do is break your neck, she told herself, and started down the still-slippery treads, easing carefully over the old gaps in the steps, watching for the new one.

She saw his trail first—a faint track wavering across the face of the slope and slightly uphill, as if something had been dragged—more a bending of weeds in one direction than actual marks in the rocky soil. It led her eye a few yards away from the stair to a low, wide clump of salal near which lay a small, defunct-looking flashlight. She thought she could make out other tracks going straight up the slope from there, but she was too far away to be sure. Following the trail in reverse back toward the stair, she spotted the new break, and moved on down to it. Now she could see the missing step, dangling by one splintered end and a few bent nails. She squatted to peer through the opening, saw a muddy snake-shape that might be a sock, and finally saw the shoe. Its tongue and canvas uppers were mauled-looking, forced open as wide as they would go, one lace broken. The instep and thick sole were still clamped between a well-anchored rock and a root as thick as her wrist. It made her teeth ache to think what it must have cost him to get his swollen foot out of there. Squeezing down through the gap between steps, she managed to put enough leverage on the root to free the shoe. Then she took both sock and shoe back up the stair, gathered the whole muddy lot together and hurried back to the house. She added them to the washer, dumped in soap, started it going, looked at her watch again. It was nearly noon.

He'd disposed of the second bowl of soup, and

was up on his elbow when she came in, looking groggy but worried. "What's that noise?" he asked as soon as he saw her.

"The washing machine, with your wardrobe in it. That's your shoes you hear thumping."

"You found my *other* shoe?"

"I did. No sweat." She put the items from his backpack on the coffee table, took the empty bowl and eased his pillows. His eyelids were drooping. "Now, listen, Jerzy. Go on to sleep. I've got to take the jeep back to the guy it belongs to, but I'll come back, on foot or horseback or somehow. In a couple hours. Because we've got to talk."

"Talk?"

"About you being here."

"Oh. Yeah." His gaze swerved away, came back to her pleadingly. "You won't tell anybody, will you?"

"Nope." Not until that plane's gone, she thought. And maybe never. Maybe *never*. She started for the kitchen.

"Hey—Girl?" She turned at the archway into the hall. He was craning to see over his cocoon. "I've still got your windbreaker."

"Doesn't matter. I'll get it later."

"Well." He blinked, focused again. "What's your name, anyway?"

That caught her unprepared. She hesitated. "Miss Piggy."

It got her the ghost of a grin. "I mean really."

"Oh, *really*. Well, really it's Princess Hannaleah-leah Uka Nuka Mauna Loa Molotov, but you can call me Hanna for short. Or Uka Nuka if you'd rather."

"Well. Thanks for the jacket. Your Majesty." He gave her another of those brief, tilted smiles and flopped back down out of her view.

"Be my guest," she told his propped-up, ice-swaddled foot. She figured he was asleep by the time she let herself out the door.

At half-past two she was again on her way up the hill that was Sandpiper Road, this time laboring on a wobbly old bike that had once been Barney's and since passed down a long succession of Cotter foster kids, becoming more battered and feeble with every one. Hanna had scorned it previously but she would have ridden a broomstick today if it had been the handiest transportation back to the Polish kid. She had never found life so interesting, nor her brain behaving so obligingly like a fireworks display. She'd spent a busy, exhilarated two hours conning this person and that with a variety of half-truths and full lies—all extemporaneous, all test-proof, all brilliant —and she confidently looked forward to a repeat performance when the need arose. Meanwhile she had swapped her pre-dinner chores for Sharon's after-dinner ones, robbed her own petty cash box, and achieved a sack of groceries, a bottle of aspirin, a pair of kids' pajamas and her own wheels. And the rest of the afternoon in which she was expected no-where.

She hid the bike under the lower deck of the house and ran up the steps to the back door with her grocery sack and bundle, buoyant as a bobbing cork. The washer was long finished; she transferred the damp wads of clothing to the dryer on her way past, hesitating over the shoes but finally tossing them in too. They began lazily thumping and bumping inside the drum as she abandoned the groceries in the kitchen and tiptoed on into the dining L and across the hall, still carrying the bundle. She peeked cautiously around the archway and met his eyes, wide-open and wary, staring directly at her. They both jumped, both giggled.

"Okay, so you're awake," she said as she walked over to him.

"I *thought* it was you. But I—" He sank back, breathing a little unevenly. He looked better, not so pale, not at all sleepy. But much more troubled. She wondered if he had a temperature. As she reached for his forehead, he took another jerky, deep breath. "Listen, Princess—Hanna or whatever it is. I want to ask you something."

"Shoot." Probably no fever, he was just upset about something.

"When—what day—are those McDowells coming home? The people who live here? I gotta know," he added urgently.

113

"Yep, I can see that might have become quite a factor in your thinking. Just all of a sudden since last night."

He was in no mood for teasing. "Well, do you know?"

"Yes. They're expected a week from tomorrow." His forehead smoothed out under her hand; as she began freeing his melted ice pack she could hear the long, relieved sigh that left his body limp and flat under the lumpy covers. "So you can relax," she added unnecessarily. "You'll have plenty of time to figure out what comes next, after that plane takes off." Leaving him to think that over, she headed for the kitchen to renew the ice in the bag.

He watched her as she came back with the fresh pack, his glance curious, only slightly wary. "What's this plane you keep talking about?"

Quite an actor, this kid. Patiently, she said, "The plane you're supposed to be climbing on this evening with your folks. There. That feel okay?"

"*I'm* supposed to be on a plane?" He was staring. "I'm not either! Anyway, how could you know anything about my folks?"

"Oh, come off it. Same way everybody in the country knows about them! And about you! I read it in the papers!"

"It's been in the *papers*? About *me*?"

"Don't give me that!" She was half-laughing, half-exasperated. But maybe he felt cornered, poor kid. More quietly, she said, "Look, Jerzy. I'm not going

114

to rat on you. But it's time for you and me to get things straight. You know what plane I'm talking about, and I know you know it. Would I be calling you by name if I hadn't tumbled to you long ago?"

He looked totally bewildered, almost scared. "You sort of nuts or something? You're *not* calling me by name. Not by *my* name. You keep calling me 'jersey.' "

"So my Polish is lousy. Come on, give up! However you're supposed to pronounce it, your name is Jerzy Stepan Wrenski, or Wrenskol, or Wrenkjold or something. Right?"

"No, it's not right! I don't know anything about Polish or Jerzy Stepan anybody. You must be out of your tree!"

He was struggling to sit up, dislodging the leg from its carefully propped pillows.

"Hey, cool it, cool it!" She caught his shoulders. "I'm not going to rat, I told you! But why lie to me, since I know already? I don't get it."

"Because it's not so! I'm not lying, it's just not so!" He sounded frustrated, exasperated, but perfectly truthful.

And suddenly she believed him.

It was like waking up by falling out of a top bunk. For a moment shock, chagrin, disorientation held her motionless, her mouth ajar. Then came outrage, as if somebody had slapped her hard across the face.

"Why, you little brat!" She shoved him back

against the pillows. "What d'you mean by . . . You're not that Polish kid at all!"

"Well, I *told* you I wasn't! I never said I *was*." His eyes had gone wide, and his voice trembled, but she was already cutting across it.

"Good lord! All that scrambling around I did— the groceries—dammit, I even scrounged you some pajamas! Risked my job . . ." She was on her feet, glaring down at him. "Who are you, then? What did you think you were doing, sneaking into this house, playing hide and seek all over the place with me—"

"I thought I was at my grandmother's!" He was blurting it out, gulping, his eyes brilliant with hurt and tears. "It's not *my* fault what you thought, is it? Why d'you have to be so meeeeeean . . ." The word wavered into the stratosphere as he flung his arm over his face.

Her anger went limp as a day-old balloon, was replaced by prickling shame. She dropped into the easy chair beside the couch. Nice going, Florence Nightingale, she told herself in disgust. Now go ahead and kick the kid on his sore foot, why don't you? "Hey, wait, Jerz—whoever you are. Wait. I'm sorry. Honest. I just . . . Please don't feel bad. I didn't mean it."

"You *did*." It was muffled by his arm, but still defiant.

"Well, yeah, I did, for a minute. I don't now. I just . . . I was so *sure*." And why? she asked herself wearily. For no reason. None at all. I just made it

116

all up. What's happening to me lately? This job must be affecting my brain or something. When she looked back at the boy he was under control again, swallowing hard, watching her unhappily, suspiciously. "So what's your name, really?" she asked. When he didn't answer she added with a touch of irritation, "Come on. You owe me that much."

"You didn't tell me yours."

"Yes I did."

"Oh. It's—Hanna, really?"

"It's Hanna really."

He hesitated only briefly. "Well, mine's Jerry. Starbeck."

She nodded. She felt tired and bruised. "Pleased to meet you, Jerry Starbeck. I guess we better start all over. What d'you say?" He was silent, gave an indeterminate shrug. "I only wish I *could*," she added. "I should've phoned my boss the minute I saw you. But no—I had to be a heroine and save you from the Commies or something. I know, I know, you don't know what I'm talking about. I'm about to show you." She got up, found Saturday's paper in the stack on the coffee table, the one with the biggest headlines: WRENSKJOLD BOY MISSING, and tossed it onto his lap as she dropped into the chair again. "Too bad they didn't have a picture. All this time I was convinced you were that Jerzy Whatsis. Don't ask me why. So now I've got a problem—you." She waited till he had absorbed the headlines and the gist of the story. Then she took

117

the paper away. "Okay. Your turn. Did we pass a grandmother back a way somewhere?"

He was frowning toward the newspaper, his mind obviously still turning over the predicament of that other boy. But he nodded, then brought his attention back abruptly to her, and the matter in hand. "This used to be my gran and grandad's house. It *did*. You can look it up if you don't believe me— Mr. and Mrs. H. L. Starbeck. I used to come here all the time when I was a little kid. A lot of it's just like I remember. There's even the same wallpaper lots of places. And I knew where the key rack was!" He felt betrayed, ill-used, you could tell by his voice—just as she had felt a few moments ago. "*I* didn't know they'd moved," he added a bit sulkily. "I saw them just last week and they never said a word."

She was beginning to feel a stirring of curiosity about him, even if he wasn't the Polish kid. "They must've moved a long time ago, Jerry. The Mc-Dowells have lived here three years."

He gave her a brief, despondent little glance that tugged at her. "Yeah, I thought maybe. I guess they just forgot I didn't know. I haven't even seen them since I was seven. Until last week."

"Where'd you see them last week? At your house?"

"No. They're my *dad's* parents. They were in Portland, on the way to California. He came and got me for lunch."

"I see. Your folks are divorced." She was beginning to get the picture—at least part of it.

118

"Yeah, and my dad was always going to bring me down here to see Gran and Grandad again, but it never worked out. *Three times* it never worked out. Mom brought me once, only about a month after we'd moved to Portland. But after the divorce she had her job—*she* couldn't . . . besides, they weren't her folks. Hers are dead," he added inconsequentially. He glanced up at her. "Are yours dead?"

"What makes you think so?"

He looked faintly surprised. "I don't know."

There was an odd little silence. But she wasn't anywhere near ready to talk about her folks yet—if ever. "It's still your turn," she reminded him. "You haven't told me much so far. You haven't told me how come you suddenly had this yen to visit your grandparents—even when they weren't at home. Even if you had to bust into the house. Even when you found somebody else's furniture all over the place."

So finally he told her—in brief, reluctant sentences. They still filled out the picture in fairly clear detail, since she knew so much of it by heart already. Grownups yanked your life all out of shape, they changed it without notice to suit themselves, they dumped you into the midst of a lot of strangers or they abruptly took you away. You felt helpless, powerless, bitter, betrayed. She'd heard this same story a dozen times, with only the names and faces changed. She'd been living it all her life.

She sighed deeply when he'd finished. "Well, join

the club. There's lots of us out here, you know. You didn't think you were something special, did you? Nope, just one of the crowd." Too bad we can't hold regular meetings, she thought frivolously. Orphans of the World, unite! Orphans and semi-orphans. You've nothing to lose but the busybodies and the unrelated siblings. We're all siblings under the skin. Oh, that's a catchy phrase. Maybe I'll grow up to be a slogan-writer. "Hey—where you going?" she said as he began struggling out of his cocoon.

"I've got to go up to the bathroom," he said with dignity.

The glance he gave her was withdrawn, slightly aggrieved. She hadn't reacted properly to his story——or maybe just not enough. He didn't like being told he was one of a crowd. Well, who did?

"There's that little john in the front hall."

"No. I want to really *wash*."

"Okay, let me help." She stood up, eased his foot off its props. "Had I better carry you? I'm all strong again now—ate my spinach while I was gone."

"I can do it."

"Suit yourself." She watched, arms folded, as he fought free of the covers and managed to hoist himself onto his good foot. Immediately he lost his balance and fell back, scowled and tried again, groping for some usable handhold. She put out her hand, caught his in time to save him from flopping back again. "Come on, I don't bite. Not hard. I'll take these pajamas along, shall I? After you have your spit bath and climb into them, you'll be more comfortable."

He muttered something but allowed her to help him hobble to the stair and up it. She saw him to the door of the pink bathroom, then wandered across the hall, dropped onto the window seat, propped her elbows on the sill, and stared out at the ocean. It was still gray and choppy, trimmed with whitecaps as far as she could see, and every tree in sight was demonstrating how it got that wind-blown shape. The sun had apparently given up until tomorrow. A better day for gulls than for strollers or sandbuckets —or fishing boats, either. The gale warnings were probably up. Fall was arriving. School next week. And that would lower the boom on Jerry once and for all.

No wonder he'd got away with his caper—nobody was worrying about him because they all thought they knew where he was. Mom thought he was with Dad, and so did those Fox kids and their Aunt Carol. Dad thought he was still with the Foxes, no doubt serenely confident that no grownup would go off and leave a twelve-year-old to his own devices. Except *him*, of course, old sweet forgivable Dad. But then he was Different, and once they all came home and he got a chance to air his excuses, they'd understand. They always had.

The bastard.

Who was it he reminded her of so vividly? Oh, yes. Mr. Blackman. The Blackmans came just before the Murchisons. Mr. Blackman was always going to take the foster kids to a real pro ball game. Only he never did.

Well, she felt for Jerry, but she was going to have to get him out of here and home, some way or other. The only problem was how to do it.

He'd managed a bath of some sort; he looked scrubbed and refreshed when he appeared in the bathroom door and stood rather sheepishly, clinging to the door jamb and holding his sore foot up, wearing Eddie Hill's pajamas.

"Not a bad fit," she commented, coming over to act as crutch.

"I had to roll up the legs and sleeves a little, is all. Who do they belong to?"

"A kid at my house who'll think he just forgot to get them into the laundry on time, as usual. He's got another pair. How's the ankle by now?"

"Not too bad. Swelling's gone down a lot."

The stairs occupied their combined attention for a while. But when he was back on the couch, foot propped, ice pack renewed, pillows plumped, cocoon discarded in favor of the lightweight afghan, he looked up at her with obvious gratitude. "Thanks, Hanna." A pause. "Sorry I was kind of snotty a while ago."

"Don't let it ruin your day," she said absently.

She sat down in the armchair near him. "Listen, Jerry. What if your mom decides to phone your dad's place to make sure you got there? Or just to see how you're doing?"

"She won't."

"What makes you so sure?"

"She never has. Anyhow she probably couldn't get hold of him. He's gone all the time."

"She'll find out sooner or later you never got there."

"She might not. They don't talk to each other unless they have to." He thought about that a minute and added, "And he doesn't even *know* Aunt Carol. Or Walter Fox."

"Oh, I see!" she said brightly. "So if you were to get home Sunday before your mom did, she'd never find out you were gone, right? She'd be too polite to ask how you sprained your ankle. And the Fox kids wouldn't even notice!"

He gave her a half-hearted grin. "Oh, well. I don't want to go home anyway."

"So what are your plans? If any?"

The last of the grin faded. "I don't have any."

She leaned forward. "Well, let me tell you something. I do. I've got plans to keep this job. It's important to me. It's very *damn* important. And I'm not going to blow it. You understand?"

"Well—sure. But—"

"But nothing. If my boss knew what I've been

winking at these past few days I'd be out on my rear end tomorrow. Which means *you've* got to be out— soon. So what'll we do?"

He swallowed. He was staring at her as if he were trying to read her mind. "What d'you mean by— soon?"

"Very *damn* soon. Where'd your grandparents move to?"

"I don't know," he said bleakly. "And anyway they're in California until after Labor Day. The eighth or ninth. If I could just find their *house*—but they're not even in the phone book here. I looked."

"Would your dad know where they'd moved to?"

"I guess so, but—" He turned to her in alarm. "You're not going to phone my dad! I won't tell you his number."

"Jerry, there can't be many Starbecks in the Portland phone book. I'll find it sooner or later, so you might as well—"

"No, wait! Wait. I've got an idea . . . only you might not want to do it."

"I'll do it! What is it? Stick up a bank? Burgle your dad's apartment?"

"I just thought—if you call him—you could pretend to be somebody else. Like maybe a friend of Gran's? Wanting to know her new address? Or something like that?"

It wasn't a bad idea at all. She stood up, a breath of hope coming in like fresh air from an open window. "Sure, why not? Who shall I be? Mrs. Martha

Whitaker. That sound about right? From—someplace far away. Chicago. Just passing through Horseshoe Beach and I thought I'd hunt up my old high school chum—D'you know your grandmother's maiden name? Her whole name?"

"Elsie Matthis Starbeck."

Hanna's thoughts paused, circled around that unhesitating answer in a kind of wonder. Elsie Matthis Starbeck—just like that. No problem. No guessing, no flights of fancy necessary. He knew. She wanted to ask if he knew his maternal grandfather's middle name, or his great-aunt's uncle's, or his third-cousin's-once-removed. But she resisted. "—my old chum Elsie Matthis. So—okay. What's his number?"

Jerry told her. Repeating it under her breath, she headed for the hall. She was already beginning to dial when she came to and slammed the phone down as if it had stung her.

"What's wrong?" Jerry called.

"It's long distance, for God's sake." Appalled, she moved back to the archway. "The charge'd show up on the McDowells' bill! And they'd call the phone company and say, 'What's this toll to Portland first week in September when I was in Timbuctu,' or wherever they are, then Samantha would call *me*, and—"

"Who's Samantha?"

"Never mind. Just remind me to use my head after this. I'll go out and find a payphone. Give me that number again." She scribbled it on the scratch pad by the phone, tore off the page, muttered a "stay put" over her shoulder and went out to the jeep. There was a phone outside the Safeway just over on White Heron Road, three minutes away.

In less than ten she was back again, tossing her battered purse on the windowseat before she turned to meet his apprehensive eyes. "Relax. All I got was a recording."

"Oh." It was a sigh of relief, tinged with disappointment. "That means he's out of town."

"For how long? The thing told me to leave my name, and he'd call back. Of course I didn't."

Jerry shrugged. "Wouldn't have done any good. Unless you were a client. A company of some kind." After a moment he added, "No telling how long he'll be away. Might be a couple days, might be a week."

"I'll try again tomorrow. I'll *keep* trying. But dammit, I wish—" Hanna broke off as another thought occurred to her. "Hey, I wonder if the post office would tell me anything?"

"I don't know."

She had a feeling it was against the law. After scanning the idea cautiously for possible risk to herself, she dialed again, cleared her throat and tried to feel like Mrs. Martha Whitaker of Chicago.

The act went down well, the voice on the other end of the line was gruff but civil, and after some hesitation bent the rules a little for her. But the news was not good. So what did you expect, a Hollywood ending? she asked herself as she wandered back into the living room and threw herself into the armchair. "They've moved up into Washington, Jerry. Your Gran and Grandad. Puget Sound area. That could be anywhere between Seattle and the Canadian border. Including a dozen islands."

Jerry sank back against his pillows, looking dashed. "He wouldn't give you the address?"

"Couldn't. Rights of Privacy law."

"And I don't know the address in California."

"So scratch the grandparents," said Hanna flatly. They eyed each other in silence. She felt panic rising in her like nausea. It blotted out everything but common sense—and fear. "Okay, that's it, Jerry. I've done what I could. You'd better tell me how to get hold of your mom."

"No, listen—wait. Dad *might* be there in a couple days—and if those McDowells aren't coming home until a week from Friday—"

"You don't have till a week from Friday. Tomorrow is more like it."

"*Tomorrow?* Oh, please could I just stay till—"

"No way. I can't risk it." She stood up, began tidying the mail stacks so she wouldn't have to meet his eyes.

"You were going to risk it for that foreign kid!"

"That was different."

"Why? Why was it different? What's so great about *him?*"

"Nothing, Jerry. But that was so much worse! Come on, you can see that. You'll only be going home—where you belong—not halfway around the world to some other country, everything different, everybody strangers, nobody even speaking your language—"

"It is not worse! All those strangers are coming to *my* house, that's the only difference. Just moving right in!"

Oh, boy. How to convince him? I've done this all wrong, Hanna thought. Why did I have to go at it like a charging rhino? Answer: because I'm scared he'll get around me. Well, he won't. I won't *let* him. It'd be insane.

She went back and sat down, took his hand awkwardly and patted it. It felt tense and reluctant in hers.

"Look, Jerry. You'll get used to those kids pretty soon, and they won't be strangers, and you might even get to like some of them. Honest. It happens. I *know*, I've had experience. And the ones you don't like you can lump. But you've got to go home."

"I don't want to, I'd have to *tell* everybody everything . . . I won't! Hanna—" His voice wavered on the word.

"Don't 'Hanna' me, I'm only doing what's got to be done! You can't stay here. You can't hack it outside, on your own. So what else is there?"

"I could stay here just till my ankle got better! Just till the McDowells come home. If you'd let me."

"Well, I won't." She dropped his hand, stood up. "I'll do one of two things. I'll phone your mom. Or

I'll phone my boss and dump it all on her. So take your choice."

She heard the harshness in her own voice, and the finality. Obviously, so did he. With an inarticulate little cry, he lurched up onto his elbow, his face twisted and his dark eyes filling.

"Then go on and phone them, I don't care! I don't care about *you*! Or anybody else! You *fink*! You're just like my dad, you make all these promises and then you chicken out! You're just—you're just—"

"I'm *not* like your dad!" She was as taken aback as if the goldfish had turned on her. "How can you say that? I didn't promise you a thing!"

"You just as good as! I thought you were my friend," he burst out bitterly.

"I am your friend! I am!"

"Well, how can I tell? You keep changing back and forth until I—" His voice quavered out of control again; he bit his lip hard.

God, what am I doing? she thought. How can I make him . . . "Jerry, listen. I don't mean to be that way! But somebody's got to do what's best for you!"

"Well, how do *you* know what's best for me? Just how? You tell me that!"

She couldn't answer. She couldn't look away from his glare, his challenge. She was as angry as he, but suddenly on the defensive, struggling to make sense of a sort of mirror-image.

But that's *my* question! she thought confusedly. He stole my line, the little fink. No, I'm the fink. He says. Well, dammit, he might be right.

Abruptly she walked away from him, over to the long windows and the long gray-on-gray horizon, with the bright goldfish in the foreground swimming their little cube of a world. She slumped onto the arm of the leather chair nearest the window, her back still to him. Surely it was best if he went home. Or was that quite the question? He'd only asked not to be sent home *now*, with his sore foot and sore feelings, to that cross-examination he'd be facing. Could anybody blame him? But that wasn't exactly the question either.

Better review the question: is this finkishness or knowing what's best for him?

Answer: Never mind. *It's best for me.*

A goldfish flicked up to the side of the tank, bumped its nose against the glass, eyes goggling at her. Don't look at *me*. I didn't put you in there, she told it bitterly.

Wearily she remembered all the times when people had known what was best for her, and she'd thought they were finks. She still thought they were finks.

She got up, walked back to the couch and stood looking down at him. "Okay, strike two. So I don't know what's best for you. You're quite a pitcher."

Slowly his face came to life. He rose up off the pillows as if pulled by cords. "You mean I can—

stay till I—till the McDowells . . . What d'you mean?"

"I mean I don't phone anybody till you say so." Her heart gave a lurch as she said it, and she sat down hard in the armchair. "I must be nuts," she added angrily. "Listen here—you've got to say so pretty soon, understand? The sooner the better. This is Wednesday already. Your mom'll be home Sunday and the lid'll blow. *So work something out.*"

"Okay," he said in rather a small voice. After a moment he added unhappily, "I guess it's not what's best for *you*."

"No. It is not. You're a damn good guesser." Okay, okay, don't take it out on him, she told herself. She leaned toward him, elbows on knees, and spoke more quietly. "We could still pull it off. So long as my boss doesn't take a notion to come check up on me. If we could get that ankle well enough so you could leave here on your own, I'd be clear out of it, see? I'd never have to admit I knew you existed. But the longer you stay, the riskier it gets."

"Yeah. I see." He looked worried but resolute. "I'll think of something. Honest. And I'll get better real fast—I'll try *hard*. I could help you around here too, you know? I could feed the goldfish. I could sort the mail!"

She managed a smile, glanced at her watch and stood up. "Just stay put and use your head. And—try not to strike me out completely."

"I promise," he whispered.

SEVEN

By Thursday afternoon Jerry's ankle looked much better. The swelling had gone down to where it seemed only a little too smooth and fat, though there were ugly purple and navy blue bruises around it like the design on an especially yucky sock.

Unfortunately it didn't *feel* much better. He had pretended it did, when Hanna was rewrapping the bandage that morning, but it still ached a lot even when he was sitting still with his foot propped up and everything as comfortable as possible. Real comfort wasn't possible. Overnight he'd discovered some other assorted bruises on his left leg and both arms, from his deliberate tumble off the steps when he was trying to reach his shoe. But he could live with those, and they didn't prevent his getting around. The ankle was something he couldn't ignore.

At least he was beginning to learn to cope with it.

He'd gone up to the bathroom that morning without waiting for Hanna's arrival, later come back down and had some cereal, negotiating the stairs by sitting his way from step to step, going backwards on the trip up and frontwards on the return, holding the leg straight out in front of him. It was tiring but it worked. Walking was harder, and far more painful even though he only touched his right foot to the floor for the bare second it took to hop forward on the left one. But when Hanna came at ten o'clock she brought a beat-up old cane she'd found somewhere at her house, and that helped a lot.

So on the hurt-ankle front he could feel he was gaining a little ground, slow as the process was. On the what-comes-next front he was nowhere. All day he'd been thinking hard about what to do, where to go, how to get himself off Hanna's hands—really trying. So far, zilch. She'd tried again to phone his dad and got the same recording, so he was no closer to locating Gran and Grandad. Unless the ankle got lots better, lots faster than it showed any signs of doing, for a while he was going to have a limp you'd notice a block away. His Mom would notice it a *mile* away—probably even over the telephone. And if he was forced to give up and go home he'd have to phone, to ask her to drive clear down here to get him. Wouldn't *that* be a great beginning for all the hard explanations and horrified questions and *more* explanations and furious phone calls to Dad when he finally got back from wherever he was, and Walter Fox knowing all about everything and *Vicky* knowing and . . .

He couldn't face it, he'd do anything first.

But he didn't want to get Hanna into trouble, or make her lose her job, which seemed extremely important to her. Hanna was a real oddball sort of girl, and she got mad awful fast, when you least expected it, and for no reason you could understand—but mostly she was nice. *Really* nice. He didn't think she was a fink now; she was playing as fair as anybody could. So he had to get out of her hair somehow.

How, how, how? Here it was four o'clock Thursday afternoon and there was only tomorrow and the next day; then it would be Sunday and Mom would be home, everybody would be home, and the egg would hit the fan. *Get better*, he raged silently at his ankle, glowering at it propped up on the opposite leather chair like a great lump of lard. He'd moved to the seaward end of the room to the funny leather chairs that sighed—and sometimes snorted—partly to have a change from the couch, partly because the view was more interesting. Not only the real view out the windows, which today was all blue skies and drifting gulls and peaceful little ice cream scoops of white cloud, but the inside view of plants and goldfish, a big improvement over a coffee table stacked with somebody else's mail. He'd played his harmonica awhile, and practiced knots for a long time, mastering the square knot and the clove hitch absolutely, and getting faster on the bowline. Then he'd watched the goldfish until he almost felt like one himself—drifting idly the length of the tank, then flicking around to drift idly back the other way, then shooting corner to corner, dodging the other two fish and weaving in and out of the little forest of water plants, then abruptly nose-diving to the bottom to hide behind the big shell—finally emerging to do the whole thing over in a different order. There was so little they *could* do, except to discover, over and over, the limits of those invisible walls. There were three fish, one pure orange-gold, one yellow-gold and smaller, one pale pinkish-white with black irregular spots like army camouflage. In Jerry's opinion, their life was stuck on dead center.

So was his, since yesterday. Earlier this afternoon, after he'd eaten the sandwich Hanna had left ready for him, and drunk some of the milk she'd brought, he'd labored his way upstairs to waste a little time with the TV. But there was nothing to watch in daytime, absolutely nothing. You had your choice of soap opera, yoga exercises, cooking instruction, or a class in art history. He watched a cartoon he'd already been tired of in the fourth grade, stood on his left foot with the right one in the bathroom washbasin for one of the five-minute hot-wet-soaks his treatment had now progressed to, and rewound the bandage. Then he labored back downstairs with another book from the corner bookcase. This one was about training your dog, only a slight improvement on the one about treasure-hunting that had put him to sleep the other day. He wondered how people like the McDowells got their books. Obviously they didn't buy them on purpose. Maybe people gave them one occasionally, or left one behind after a visit, and they just kept putting them in that bookcase. Jerry longed for some of the good science fiction he had in his room at home, or even the old adventure stuff he kept at Dad's.

Dad. He wondered where Dad was, where Dad thought *he* was. Every time he thought of Dad he felt a pain—far worse than the pain in his ankle because it was far down inside, and not likely to go away, maybe ever. What's more, he thought about him several times a day. He couldn't seem to help it. Like right now, at the end of a long, long afternoon with his eyes again hypnotized by the goldfish and his spirits at a low enough ebb already, here he was thinking about Dad. Desperately he wrenched his mind away, found his harmonica and started running through the old tunes Grandad had taught him that long ago Christmas day when the harmonica was new. By now he could almost play them backwards, and they usually untied inner knots. Today they only made him lonesome for Grandad. He tried to think about Hanna instead—someone new, someone hopeful. He began to long for Hanna to come.

It was then he got his idea—the best, in fact the

only one he'd come up with for what to do about all this.

He would just go home with Hanna! Stay at her house instead of here. Why not? It wouldn't be for long, only until his ankle got better. She could tell her mom he was a friend's brother, and the friend was away, or . . . anyway, she'd think of something. There must be several kids at her house—as witness these pajamas—and parents with lots of kids never seemed to notice one or two extra. Now if it were *his* mom . . . But at Hanna's house probably nobody'd mind at all. So why wouldn't that work?

If Hanna would do it. That was the only part he didn't know about. One of the many things he didn't know about Hanna.

A quarter-hour later she walked through the living room archway, and he plunged right into it—announcing, then uneasily explaining, then adding hasty afterthoughts—and all the time feeling his confidence drain away under the startled scrutiny of those sharp green eyes. But when he finally stumbled to a halt with a lame apology for sort of inviting himself, she looked more amused than angry.

"Jerry, it's no go. Sorry. Nothing wrong with the idea—or with your asking, either. But it's not my house."

"Oh." His brief glow of hope went out like a candle. Not her house. "You mean you live with somebody else?" An uncle and aunt, he supposed. Or grandparents. A little crossly he said, "If you live there, it's *sort* of your house, isn't it?"

She gave a hoot of laughter. "Tell that to Mrs. Arne Cotter. Her own son's been paying board since he was about fourteen. And the rest of us—" She stopped, waved that away with a sigh. "There's lots of somebody-elses, Jerry. Seven people in a *small* three-bedroom house. The place is so jammed you can see legs and arms sticking out the windows when we're all there."

"It's a boarding house?" Jerry was floundering.

She didn't answer for a minute. "I guess you could say that. No, the hell you could. We're foster kids, Jerry. The Cotters get paid to keep us. And believe me, they'd never keep anybody five minutes *without* getting paid."

Foster kids. "Orphans, you mean?" Jerry said hesitantly.

"Orphans. Full or semi. I mean, some kids have a parent alive but just not on the scene any longer— like Sharon. Anyhow we couldn't wedge you in. So scratch the whole idea."

Jerry was silent, staring at her snub-nosed profile. He'd never known any orphans, or even semi-orphans. He'd known some divorced kids, like himself, but all of them lived with at least one parent. He felt as if she'd told him her house was full of amputees. Awkwardly he ventured, "Don't you want to talk about it?"

"Not specially." She got up from the arm of the chair with an irritable movement that made her hair bounce. It was crisp, turned-up hair that kept reminding Jerry of the carrot-curls his mother used to make when she had a party. It was brighter than carrots, though—more the color of that biggest goldfish. She had really neat hair; it was hard to quit looking at it—especially when she had her back to you. But then she turned, and there was that round, homely face with a too-wide mouth and too-white skin dappled with pale orange freckles. And the narrow green eyes, sardonic again as she turned to survey him through their light lashes. "I suppose I'd better, though, or you'll be imagining God knows what. You got questions?"

Jerry did have questions, but right then he was busy having feelings—surging, unexpected feelings of fierce loyalty to Hanna, and being *sorry* she was an orphan, and liking her enormously whatever she looked like. For a second he was too full of feelings to think of questions at all. But he swallowed, and chose one at random. "Who's Sharon?"

"My current roommate. She's eight years old. Right now at Cotters' there's Sharon and me in the little bedroom, and Tony and Eddie-whose-pajamas-you're-wearing in Barney's room with Barney. And of course the Cotters in their room. The roll call changes, but there's always four of us besides the family at any one time. Sometimes five, if they can

139

get one young enough to sleep in a crib in the living room. I'm the oldest of this batch." Hanna paused. "I'm almost always the oldest."

"Why?"

She shrugged. "Most kids get adopted long before they get to my age. I didn't."

"Well, how come?" demanded Jerry belligerently.

"Oh, it just happens sometimes. Nobody took to me, I guess."

Jerry's heart swelled. He could hardly breathe all of a sudden. "Well, I'd've adopted you first thing!" he burst out. "I'd've picked you out of the whole orphanage—" He stopped because she was laughing at him, her eyes wide with surprise. "Well, I would," he mumbled, going hot with embarrassment.

"Don't waste your sympathy," she told him, but with a quick touch on top of his head that made him feel better.

She was perched again on the arm of the opposite leather chair, still wearing her windbreaker. She looked very impermanent.

"Do you have to go right away?" Jerry asked pleadingly.

"Not really. You want me to stay awhile?"

"Can you? I get so *bored*."

She stood up, shucked off the windbreaker and tossed it aside. "Well, I don't do slide lectures or tap dancing. How does a hot soak for the foot grab you as entertainment?"

"I soaked it once this afternoon—right after

140

lunch. Boy, there's *nothing* on the TV daytimes. And *nothing* to read. And I've tied knots till I'm cross-eyed."

"So that's why you had that cord in your pocket. Can you do a manger tie?"

"No. What's that?" Jerry felt a flicker of interest. But Hanna was on her way to the kitchen. "I'll show you while you soak."

Once she had the newspapers spread, and the bath towel over the papers, and the dishpan full of hot water on the towel, she unwound the undershirt-bandage, and examined the foot with critical approval. "I like your color scheme. Okay, dunk it. Where's that cord?"

Jerry fished it out from between the seat cushion and the back of the chair and tossed it to her as he eased his foot gingerly into the steaming water. "*Wow*. When you say hot you mean hot!"

"No sense fooling around. Now you've got this horse, see, and you want to hitch him to a fence post for a minute while you find out if he's really lame on his off hind foot or just kidding you. All right, you take the rope *around* the post, and *under* itself—"

"How come you know so much about horses?" asked Jerry in astonishment. That didn't fit with his idea of orphans and foster homes at all.

"Stayed on a farm six months when I was thirteen. Pay attention. *Around* the post, then *under* itself. Then you double the free end into a loop, see, like this—and put that loop through the first loop you already have there. Then tighten 'er up and the harder that horse sets back, the tighter he's tied. When you want to *untie*, you just pull the free end —and there you are."

"Hey, neat!" Jerry reached for the cord and tried it himself, around the post of the table lamp she'd been using, which she obligingly pushed closer. It was an easy knot to learn, and wonderfully efficient. "Did you like the farm?" he ventured.

She hesitated. "I liked the *farm*. I went ape over the horses. I liked the cats and the barn and stuff like that."

"But—?" Jerry studied her profile warily. It was remote and uninviting. You could never tell when Hanna was going to go off unexpectedly, like a firecracker.

"Oh, the people were kind of stinkers. At least the farmer was, and this son they had, kid about eighteen—what a jerk!"

"What happened?" Jerry said breathlessly.

He was suddenly being looked at—and through —by those shrewd, amused green eyes. "What is this, Thriller Hour? Nothing happened. Nothing that had much to do with me. But the first thing you learn if you're a foster kid is that if *anything* goes wrong, you can start packing. Is that water cooling off too much?"

"No, for cripe's sake. It's just getting comfortable."

"Well, it ought to be uncomfortable. I'll get the kettle."

He watched her cross the room toward the kitchen, walking fast as usual, whistling under her breath. She wasn't unlike a horse herself—a skinny young one like those leggy colts at Marshs', next to Dad's place at the lake. They looked so awkward and uncertain until they moved, then everything worked like water flowing. He wondered if he ought to ask her anything else about herself. She kept changing the subject, he noticed. But when she came back and began cautiously adding hot water to the dishpan, curiosity won.

"Hanna?"

"Um."

"Do *you* have a parent living but just not on the scene any longer? Like that Sharon? Or are yours both dead?"

"No idea."

"What? But you must know whether they're—"

"I don't know a thing about 'em. They could be living next door for all I know. Or running the pool hall down town. Or serving ninety-nine and a half years for first-degree murder." She glanced at him, smiled a little at his open mouth, and added, "Or dead. I guess I prefer that, on the whole."

"But—somebody must've brought you to the orphanage."

"Jerry, there aren't any orphanages nowadays. You're thinking of Oliver Twist or something." Hanna straightened up, took the kettle over and set it on the hearth, came back and settled herself in the other leather chair, which wheezed asthmatically as it eased her down. "Okay, you want the whole wild and exciting story, I can tell. The character who brought me to the County Children's Services office was an old biddy who said her name was Bessie—as near as anybody could make out. She was almost too drunk to carry me, much less talk without her teeth. I was about three at the time, and she was about seventy-five, or maybe a hundred and five. She said she was a sort of step-grandmother. Whatever that means. She knew my name—or maybe invented it. She might have been a neighbor, heard a baby crying and went and took it home the way you would a kitten. I guess she'd had me a couple of years. Nobody ever unraveled the bit about where she got me in the first place. It was obvious why she wanted to get rid of me. One foot in the grave and barely enough money for booze as it was. So we said a fond farewell which I don't remember—fortunately I don't remember her, either—and the county became my guardian. End of story."

Jerry stared at her in silence, trying to picture her as a helpless three-year-old, with freckles and carrot-curl hair and sharp green eyes and . . . no. He couldn't make her anything but Hanna, and he couldn't imagine her as helpless. She probably kicked that old Bessie in the ankle whenever she was hungry. "It's not either the end of the story," he said. "It's the beginning."

"Oh, well—the rest is simple. Like an old TV series rerun. I was put in a foster home. Then I was put in another foster home. Then I was put in *another* foster home. Shall I go on?"

He grinned, but really it sounded kind of interesting. Living all those different places, with all those different kids—and on a farm once, with horses. You wouldn't have time to get bored. "I don't see much wrong with all that. I think it'd be fun. At least things kept *happening* to you." He felt suddenly dissatisfied with his uneventful life. "Nothing much has ever happened to me."

"Until now."

He'd forgotten about Now. "Yeah, until now," he muttered.

After a moment's silence, she leaned over and tested the temperature of his footbath, said, "Maybe we've boiled that long enough. Looks done to me." She hoisted the foot up, flipped a bath towel around it and laid it gently on the seat of the other leather chair, dropping the strips of undershirt in his lap. "Sort of roll those up and we'll put 'em back in the rag bag. I got you an elastic one at the drugstore for your very own. I'll get it after I empty this." She headed for the kitchen with the dishpan.

Jerry didn't answer. He was feeling as if a load of bricks had just settled around his shoulders. He wished she hadn't *mentioned* Now. He didn't speak when she came back and began swaddling up his

145

heat-reddened, purple and navy blue ankle, but sat brooding, winding and unwinding the undershirt strips around his hand.

"I'm sorry, Jerry. I know this thing hurts pretty bad still. And it really complicates your life, doesn't it?"

He waved that away impatiently. "The ankle's *nothing*. It's—all the other. The Foxes. Everything's going to be different. *Everything*."

She fastened the safety pin. "So everything'll be different. You just got through saying you thought that'd be fun. Things happening to you."

"I didn't mean *this* kind of thing. This is permanent." It came over Jerry again, the irreversibility of it, his helplessness. "I won't be able to get *rid* of those Fox kids. I've *got* 'em. Forever!"

She stood looking down at him a minute, then wandered over to the window and stood watching the ocean, one knee on the window seat and her hands in her pockets. "Is that so bad? That's what I've always wanted. To *keep* somebody—almost anybody. For permanent."

"But . . . but what if I don't *like* 'em?"

"What if you do? You might be nuts about 'em. You don't really know one way or the other yet, do you?"

"No, but—"

She swung around toward him. "Let's say you *don't* like 'em. So the world won't end. And nobody's going to kick you out. You're going to stay

146

put, have your same room, your same mom. Your *real* mom. You know exactly what she's like and all about her—you even know your granmother's middle name, for God's sake! What're you complaining about?"

She was beginning to spark and flash a little. Jerry eyed her warily. "I won't have my real *dad*. I'll have that Walter Fox—"

"Well, he might be an improvement! From what I've heard of your real dad. And by the way I tried to call him again and he's *still* not home." She whirled around, jerked open a drawer in the table between the two leather chairs. "Want to play double-sol?"

"Double-sol?" He gaped at her.

"Double-solitaire. You know, a game. With cards. Come on, we need something to do besides yak at each other. Is there a pencil on that coffee table?"

So for a while they played double-sol whether Jerry especially wanted to or not. Grudgingly at first, then with growing absorption because you had to keep your wits about you to play with Hanna, he got his mind off Foxes and onto cards and numbers, actually managing to win a game by the skin of his teeth. It was Hanna who seemed unable to divert her thoughts. Absently shuffling the cards and letting him figure the scores unaided, she said suddenly, "You know what? I'll bet he's scared to death of you. This Walter Fox."

147

"Scared of *me*?"

"Why not? You can make his life a misery. Turn your mom against him. Bug his kids till they give *him* a bad time for blowing everything."

"He'd just take their side. He told Tom he could ride my bike, and—"

"Likely Tom was drumming his heels and turning purple at the prospect of taking on a big brother, when he's already got two sisters bossing him around. And what about that Vicky? She's always been oldest. Now *you* are. What's more she's saddled with a new mom she never asked for. I'll bet my next week's pay she's worrying more about your mom right now than you are about her dad."

"Then she's dumber than I thought!" Jerry retorted. "My mom is nice."

"Nice enough to side with Vicky in a showdown? If the hassle was your fault?"

"Well, sure! Of course!" Jerry regarded her crossly, feeling a bit startled and wondering just how sure he was. He didn't really know how his mother would react to a hassle. She wasn't used to hassles. She was used to just one kid, and hearing his side of everything and his sometimes pretty slanted version of the other side, and after trying hard to weigh the two, usually ending up deciding he was right. And often he wasn't, but it made him feel better anyway, and made it easier, later, to admit he might have been wrong. It worked very well, that system. It hadn't ruined his character at all. It was these Foxes who were going to ruin his character, and his disposition too. The very thought of his mom taking Vicky's part against *him* made the heat come up inside him and his teeth clench hard. How could Hanna think of such a thing? "Whose side are you *on*?" he demanded.

She smiled briefly. "Yours, Jerry. Honest. But I've stood where Vicky's standing, so many times . . ."

"Well, she doesn't need to worry! Deal."

With disarming meekness, Hanna dealt. But as they were laying out their cards she said absently, "What's she like, this Vicky? How does she act around you? Smile a lot? Laugh? Offer a lot of conversation?"

"Vicky?" Jerry stared at her. "No! She never says much at all unless she's cutting down one of the others. She never smiles, either. Or much of *anything*. She usually reads a book." He visualized the back of Vicky's mussed blonde head in the car, stiff-necked, turned straight front, the green plastic barrette holding the wilted rose. And later, the face raised occasionally from the book—guarded, remote. "I don't know what she's like," he admitted.

"So maybe no news is good news," Hanna remarked.

"I'd just as soon not find out anyhow," he told her sulkily. He was tired of being preached at. Hanna didn't *know*, that was all. He put a Jack on her ten, completed one of his stacks, and said, "Your turn."

They finished the game—which Hanna won—but

instead of shuffling again she glanced at her watch and then put the cards in their box and the box in the table drawer, saying she had to go upstairs and water the plants in the bedroom. "Forgot 'em this morning. Too busy looking after you."

Her voice was flippant, and Jerry knew she didn't mean it, but it made him feel guilty anyhow, and suddenly ashamed of his crabbiness. Hanna was doing a lot for him, after all, he thought remorsefully as he watched her cross the room, whistling, and swing around the archway on her way upstairs. Buying groceries out of her own pocket, and elastic bandages and things. And he wasn't giving much in return but backtalk and gripes about the Foxes. That was a pretty crummy way to act; his mom would chew him out if she knew. The Foxes weren't Hanna's problem. *He* was Hanna's problem—and a constant threat to her job. And he'd done nothing to solve that, either.

Again he wondered what was so special about this job, why it was so important to her. This morning he'd even asked her. But she'd only said it fit into any odd hour of the day, so you could hold down another job as well, and have two pay checks instead of one. Which didn't explain much, because he didn't think she had another job. There'd be no time to work at it, what with coming out here twice a day to check on him. It dawned on him that he might have loused up her other job already—just by needing her. Acutely uncomfortable, he listened to her footsteps, light and brisk, moving about overhead and trotting down the stairs, and when she came through the archway he asked her straight out what other job she'd been talking about this morning.

"Oh, that. I was shucking crabs four hours a day down at the Cotters' fish store. I'm surprised your nose didn't tell you that right away."

Was shucking crabs. Past tense. "You don't smell fishy that I ever noticed," Jerry mumbled.

"Well, I did all summer. Maybe I've aired out some by now."

"You mean you don't do it now. They fired you, didn't they?" Jerry burst out. "Because of me."

She turned to stare, then crossed the room to him. "*No.* What put that in your head? They found a girl who can work weekdays in winter. I've got to go back to school next week."

"Oh," Jerry murmured, feeling vastly relieved and a little silly. Nothing to do with him at all—why did he always think he was so important? He glanced up self-consciously to find her still studying him, frowning. She eased down beside his propped-up leg in the other leather chair.

"Listen, don't worry about me," she commanded. "I'm just fine. I still do the crabs on Saturdays, and the house-sitting goes on all winter. When the Mc-Dowells get home, I'll start checking somebody else's house. Samantha might give me two or three regulars once the summer people start closing their beach places. She pays me five bucks per week per house. I'll get where I'm going, don't you doubt it." She finished with an emphatic bob of her head.

So that's who Samantha was—her boss. Five bucks a week—two or three times. It was a lot of money to earn in just odd moments of the day or evening. Jerry began to understand about the job. Diffidently, he asked, "Where *are* you going? I mean—are you saving up for something?"

"You're damn right I am." She leaned forward, propping her forearms on her knees to fix him with a gleaming green gaze. "The minute I get one thousand bucks I'm moving out of Cotters'. Out of foster homes. Forever and ever amen."

"You mean—right away? Not finish high school?"

"I can do that any old time. You just take some tests."

"But where'll you go? What'll you—"

"I'll go down the coast, California maybe. To some bigger place, where I can get a job I can live on."

"What kind of job?"

"Any kind! Feeding the elephants. Painting the Golden Gate Bridge!"

Jerry giggled a bit nervously. He felt half awed, half scared, at the boldness of the plan. "But will they let you?"

"The county? They'll be glad to get rid of me. I

cost 'em two hundred and fifty bucks a month. Anyhow, it's okay after you're sixteen, if you think you can hack it. And once you finish high school, you're on your own anyway. That's the end of the line for foster kids."

Jerry took a long breath, conjuring up a mental picture of Hanna climbing up a girder on the Golden Gate Bridge. It was no trouble at all. "When d'you figure you'll—do all this?"

"Maybe after Christmas. I was hoping I'd make it this summer, but I still need a couple hundred dollars, maybe more. I'm kind of scared to leave without my thousand. There'll be room rent, and I've got to eat..."

She fell silent, staring past him at some mental picture of her own. Jerry tried to join her in it, but got no further than a small bare room, a table with one TV dinner. "Won't you be lonesome?" he asked softly.

There was a long pause. Hanna shifted her gaze to him, with no change of expression. "Yeah, maybe. Probably." She shrugged. "I guess there's lots worse things than being lonesome." Abruptly she skewered him with one of her sharp glances. "You ought to know. You've always been the only kid—weren't you ever lonesome?"

"Why—well, I—" Jerry was suddenly remembering his bitter longing, only three days ago, for just one cousin, just one kid really related to him.

"Sometimes, I guess. But not for Foxes," he added with a sharp glance of his own. "I wouldn't mind if *you* came to live at my house."

"What a soft-soaper." Hanna grinned and put her feet up in the chair beside him.

"No, honest. Or if . . ." Jerry stopped, his breath suddenly leaving him. Then he wriggled up off his backbone in the slippery chair. He was having an idea so startling that he could only stare at it in wonder for a minute, expecting to see it pop like the rainbow-colored soap bubble it seemed and vanish, leaving a mere puddle of impossibilities. But it didn't pop, and it didn't vanish. Slowly he transferred his stare to Hanna. "Listen . . . hey, listen, Hanna, why don't we *both* do what you said? Take off for California? Now, tomorrow! It'd solve everything—"

"Oh, very funny."

"No, wait! Let me tell you!" Swiftly, as lucidly as possible when he was stuttering with excitement, he outlined his plan, which seemed more sensible, more workable, every minute. They'd get him some crutches so he could travel. Then they'd climb on a bus, go wherever she decided, find a place to live, and a job for her, and once his ankle was well *he'd* get a job too, on Saturdays and after school—and they'd take some other name like Smith or Jones, and pretend to be brother and sister, and live together and be each other's family. And of course later when he was in high school—

"Jerry, *stop*." Half laughing, she reached across their lined-up legs and felt his forehead.

He jerked away impatiently. "I'm not delirious or anything!"

"You've lost your mind. I told you—I don't have enough money saved yet to keep myself in second-hand jeans—much less take on a dependent."

"But *I've* got some."

That stopped her. Jerry watched with satisfaction as her expression changed from amusement to sudden attention. "You've got some what?" she asked carefully.

"Money! I've got a savings account! I forgot it—" Cripes sake, Jerry was thinking frustratedly, why didn't I think of it way back on Monday when I found out Gran had moved—when I could've *used* it to get out of here—I wouldn't even have sprained my ankle . . .

But he wouldn't have known Hanna, either.

"Will you go *on*?" she burst out irritably. But she only half believed him still—he could tell. "You have a savings account but you forgot it. I wish you'd tell me how anybody could forget a thing like that."

Feeling stupid and apologetic, he explained it. His mother had started the account soon after her divorce; *she* always put the money in, *she* kept track of whatever you kept track of. He'd never had much to do with it. It was for his college, or emergencies, only there hadn't been any, and college was such a

155

long way off he never thought of this as money he could *spend*—

But the tension had gone out of her as he talked; she was smiling, an oddly un-Hanna-like expression on her freckled face. "Jerry, you're a really great kid. You really are. I can't tell you how much I'd like to go off somewhere with you and be each other's family."

"Well, then—!"

"—But that's *not* money you can spend. That savings account'll be in your mom's name too. She'd have to countersign the checks. How old were you when she opened it?"

"I dunno. About five, I guess. But—"

"Well, see? Nobody in their right mind—"

"But it's *not* in her name. Not now. She *told* me. So that if anything happened to her I could *get* it. Here, hand me that backpack!" Without waiting, he twisted across her outstretched legs and reached it himself, fished out his wallet and flipped it open to display the proof—a plastic card plainly labeled "Savings Account Identification Card," with a long number and one name only on it—his.

Hanna might have turned into a Hanna-shaped cookie or something, sitting there staring with no expression except a slightly dazed one. "You mean it's *real?*" she asked him in a strange voice.

"Yes! I keep telling you! It's real. All I've got to do is take this card to our bank—or any branch of it—and they'll give me the money."

"How—how much is there? Probably not much," she added swiftly.

"Well—I don't know." That made him feel like a dumb little kid again. "I could probably figure it out. She's always put in thirty dollars a month."

Hanna's eyes flew wide. "Since you were five years old? With compound interest?"

Abruptly she was out of the chair, across the room to the little writing desk beyond the fireplace, where she snatched up something and began to poke it. A calculator, it must be—Jerry hadn't noticed it before but you only poked that way at calculators or push-button telephones. He wondered if Hanna could do compound interest on top of everything else.

But she was only human too; she was muttering, "I won't even bother with the interest, but—Jerry, how old are you?"

"I was twelve last month."

"So minus five that's seven years, times twelve months a year, times thirty bucks a month—" A pause while she stared at whatever showed on the calculator, then turned the pale oval of her face toward him. "Jerry—that's twenty-five hundred and twenty dollars right *there*. Without figuring the interest at all!"

And it was enough, more than enough, Jerry could tell just from the weightless way she was standing, still clutching the calculator—like something that was going to be airborne in the next ten seconds. Excitement rushed up in him and nearly choked him. "So are we going to do it? Hanna? Are we?"

The ten seconds ticked by, almost audibly, like heartbeats, while he held his breath and Hanna didn't move so much as an eyelash. Then, slowly, the airiness drained out of her; he saw it go, saw her become earthbound and droop-shouldered again, and she slung the calculator back on the desk with a scornful clatter.

"No, of course we're not going to do it, are you out of your skull? Even if I'd rip off your college money—which I won't—how long d'you think we'd get away with a caper like that? About five minutes. Once your mom walks in that house Sunday and finds you gone she's going to start raising hell all over the place. She'll call your dad, then she'll call the cops, then they'll call the state police. You know what? We're a couple of morons and I don't know which one's worse, you or me."

She sank onto the desk chair as if her knees had caved in under her. Jerry, feeling as if she'd just knocked him down and stepped on him, watched her through a trembling blur that stung his eyes and hurt his throat. After several tries he got his jaw muscles untied enough to bring a few words out, in strangled tones. "I don't see what's so dumb. About it. We could try. We could change our names. It *might* work."

"It *won't* work. And we're not trying." Hanna

stood up wearily, lifted her wrist as if it weighed a ton and looked at her watch. "I've got to get out of here."

She's going to walk out on me. She never meant any of it. She was just *lying*! . . . Jerry knew he was being unreasonable and didn't care. He saw what it was. She wanted to go, all right—and she wanted the money. She just didn't want *him* along. Well, she needn't think he didn't catch on. Rigidly controlling his voice, he said distantly, "Okay. If you don't want to. *I* don't care."

He turned away carelessly, stared toward the ocean. A moment later her bright head was between him and the view. She hunkered down level with him and looked him straight in the eye. He had to look back at her—and he saw he was wrong.

"Jerry," she said. "You'll never know how much I want to. And we're going to forget the whole ball of wax right this minute, quick, before we do something godawful stupid." She stood up, started swiftly toward the kitchen. "I brought you a pizza for dinner. I hope you like pepperoni."

After a long, soul-easing moment and a longer breath, he was able to call out something about pepperoni being his favorite. She wasn't walking out, she did want him along, she felt exactly the way he did. It was going to be okay. Because sooner or later she'd give in, and they'd go. It was the way out—and they both knew it.

159

EIGHT

Hanna drove up Sandpiper Road next morning
wishing she'd never heard of Jerry's bank account.
Or Jerry, either. She'd had a bad night of it, telling
herself crossly, over and over, that his cockeyed
plan would never work, and anyway she couldn't
and wouldn't take his money. But a treacherous
inner voice kept insisting that it *might* work, that
she'd only be *borrowing* the money—just a small
part of it—for just a short while.

At three o'clock in the morning she'd crawled out
of bed, stealthily so as not to wake Sharon, who was
a light sleeper, and groped in the dark for her slip-
pers and her old quilted robe. Struggling into them,
she'd sneaked down the hall to the living room, not
quite managing to avoid the squeaky board, and let
herself silently out the front door. The moon was
almost full, dodging in and out among swift-moving

clouds and casting a dappled, kaleidoscopic light over the few scraggly bushes, the patch of lawn, the three cracked cement steps leading down to the walk from a porch that sloped a little more to the left every day. The street was empty, the small houses crowded along it were dark and withdrawn. Hanna sat down on the top step and hugged her knees and told herself again it would never work.

But that busy inner voice was plotting the details. They could take another name, as Jerry had said— pretend to be brother and sister—she could easy pass for eighteen if she had to. They could take a bus down the coast, to one of those towns like Santa Rosa or Santa Fe—no, that was someplace else. San Jose? Anyhow, some town big enough to hide in, small enough to cope with. Or it might be better to go inland, to the valley where they grew all the lettuce and stuff. She'd heard there were always transients around those places, picking crops— Fresno? Was that one of them?—and nobody would notice a couple more . . .

You dreamer, she told herself caustically. You idiot. Brother and sister! There's about as much family resemblance as you'd find between a cat and a dog. That blows the whole thing right there, can't you use your head?

He could easy be your half-brother, whispered the inner voice. *Nobody's going to be asking for your birth certificate.*

"Oh, shut up, dammit!" she muttered. She sprang

to her feet, walked down the steps and once around the shadow-blotched yard, kicking at a forgotten bicycle pump, a flat-sided basketball, repudiating the inner voice and all its works, reminding herself just where she'd stand if—*when*—their little caper was discovered. It was all right for Jerry, he had nothing to lose—when things went bust he'd simply go home to his loving mother. But *she'd* wind up in the clink or something. She had no idea what they'd do to her—maybe lock her up as insane, which she very likely was, to consider this harebrained notion for more than twenty seconds. She stumbled over a broken tricycle and finally gave up and returned to the steps—to find Barney looming, bearlike, in the black rectangle of the doorway.

"Oh, for the love of—! Go back to bed!" she told him in an exasperated undertone.

"Not sleepy right now." He came out, easing the door to behind him, and lowered his big hulk onto the top step. The maroon robe he'd inherited from his Grampa Cotter was a full size too small. "Something's bothering you, Red. Noticed it at dinner. Better tell old Barney."

Hanna made a brief, rude noise and dropped down on the step below him. "Stay out of my life. There's nothing to tell."

"I don't want to stay outa your life," he said patiently. "I wanta get in it. But if you don't want to tell me, that's okay."

They sat in silence, Barney placid, forearms on

162

angled knees and hands loosely clasped between them—Hanna coiled like a spring. She was wondering, desperately, if this time she should let go all holds, just step out of the airplane, and tell old Barney. Trusting the parachute to open. Trusting Barney, as he was always wishing she would do. Barney was canny—he might come up with some sort of sensible solution if she could bring herself to hand over the whole secret from the beginning. But it was Jerry's secret, as well as her own. And Barney didn't know or care about Jerry.

No. Don't do it, don't do it, she told herself, feeling a shiver of fright at how close she had come to it. This time Barney wouldn't come through for her. He'd shoot down that woolly-headed scheme on sight, knowing it was doomed before it started. Then he'd call her a damn fool—gently—for letting the kid stay in that house five minutes, and point out the trouble she was courting with everybody from Samantha to the law, to let him stay even five minutes longer. Then he'd get Jerry out of there, sprained ankle and all, and back to his mom. And he'd say he was only doing what was best for them both.

And he'd be right—on all counts.

"Red?" Barney's voice came questioningly from the step above. She felt a big hand touch her shoulder. "You're gonna bust your mainspring if you don't relax. You're so uptight you're beginning to vibrate."

"You just forget about my mainspring. I'll unwind it myself," Hanna told him. She released her grip on her knees, renewed her inner, leechlike suction on sixteen years of experience, and stood up, stiff and chilled. "I'm going back to bed whether you've got sense enough to or not. G'night." She padded across the sagging porch, quietly let herself in, then hesitated. Looking back at the big silent figure still sitting on the steps in his hand-me-down robe, she sighed. "Thanks anyway, Doc," she added.

Now, driving up the last rise of Sandpiper Road, she was glad she'd kept her mouth shut. For Barney, this would have been the crunch. All *he* wanted was whatever was best for her, and he'd have turned fink to see that she got it, whether she wanted it or not. He'd say she ought to do the same for Jerry. The difference was, *she* didn't want what was best for Jerry, any more than Jerry did.

One thing was certain—she wasn't going to push and shove. Jerry had to see it himself. He'd conned her into letting him make all the decisions so far— let him make this one. She'd have all she could handle just keeping neutral.

So where does that leave me? she thought as she turned into the drive. Right where I was—in the middle.

On her way past the little Horseshoe Beach library she'd stopped and checked out a couple of books—one science fiction, one about knots. She tucked them under her arm and went in the house.

The living room was empty. From what seemed far in the distance the thin voice of the harmonica wailed faintly, tracing some plaintive little tune. She listened a moment, then tossed the books on the couch and headed down the narrow stairs to the art room. Mighty adventurous he was getting, on that wooden leg.

She found him outside on the back deck in the sunshine, standing on his good foot and leaning on the railing, with Grampa Cotter's scarred old cane, long an indistinguishable part of the clutter in the Cotters' hall closet, hanging beside his elbow. Against the sweep of sky and ocean he looked small and alone. The tune turned out to be "Turkey in the Straw," hardly a tearjerker, but that harmonica could make "Yankee Doodle" sound like an attack of the dismals.

She reached his side as he finished, surprising him into a startled "Yikes!" and a grab at the railing. "Cripes sakes! I didn't know you were anywhere around!"

"I didn't think *you* were, at first. How'd you get clear down here?"

"Oh, it wasn't much harder than the other stairs. Then I walked, with just the cane." He was proud of himself. "See? I could travel, easy. I don't need crutches."

"Travel home, you mean."

"Travel to *California*. Hey, Hanna—have you been—you know—thinking?"

"Me? What about?"

"*You* know. My new idea."

"Oh. No, I guess I sort of forgot that. You play that thing pretty well, for a beginner. How about another number?"

He gave her a look, a shrug that said he had more time and patience than she had, and began a loud and spirited rendition of "You're in The Army Now." Where did he get these antiques? They reminded her of the tunes Mrs. Murchison's old uncle used to play on his concertina. This one managed to sound doleful too. "While you're busy with the funeral I'm going up to do my chores," she cried above the noise, and left him to it. The longer she could get him to concentrate on that instead of her, the better.

She wondered just exactly how he was picturing this marvelous life of theirs in California. Probably as some non-stop game of play-acting, featuring a perfectly convincing brother and sister named Smith or Jones living in a comfortable, well-ordered little house not bothering anybody or being bothered. A life just like his usual one, in fact, with her substituting for his mom . . . Not that I know one crying thing about his usual life, or whether it's all that comfortable and well-ordered or not, she reminded herself as she filled the watering pot.

All the same, the kid was sound asleep and dreaming. If she could just find a way to wake him up—really wide awake—she had a notion he'd run for home. *Then* how would you feel? she demanded of herself.

She considered that briefly as she carried the pot into the living room, remembered she'd watered everything yesterday, and carried it back to empty it. The answer, without any doubt, was that she'd feel terrible. She'd miss him like an arm or leg.

Oh, come off it, she told herself crossly. A kid you've known less than a week?

But that wasn't how it felt—it felt as if she'd known him forever. Which was idiotic, when you considered that much of his life was a blank in her mind. To her he was a figure on an empty stage, with no one in the wings except a few wraiths named Grandad and My Mom and Walter Fox. Yet he seemed completely knowable, completely hers.

That was the headache, she thought as she crumbled the food over the fish tank and watched the three swift forms flash up, bright iron filings to a magnet. He wasn't just *a* kid, he'd somehow become *her* kid. Partly because that ankle had got them playing Truth or Consequences before they knew each others' names. Mostly because from the beginning he'd needed so much from her—at first only her silence and a blind eye; now, everything. What's more she'd come through for him—uncharacteristically and at considerable risk to herself. Why did I do that? she asked herself, bewildered. How did I *get* here, all involved up to my armpits?

She sank into one of the sighing leather chairs, watching the transports of the fish over their uninteresting goodies, and tried out some answers. *Because of Jimmy, all those years ago. Because I need somebody too—I've been on that empty stage all my life. Because I like him. Because you can't change a kid's ice packs and haul him up and down stairs and cut his muddy jeans off him without winding up feeling he belongs to you.*

Maybe it was that simple, really. Nurses probably felt that way about their patients.

Oh, sure. And clung to them, bawling, when they were due to leave the hospital.

Well, never *mind* why. She'd feel like hell if she lost him. Or would she just feel like hell if she lost her chance at that bank account?

She heaved herself up out of the leather chair, which gave its usual gasp of relief, and started out to get the mail, wondering if there were any embezzlers in her unknown family. The temptation to get her hands on that savings account seemed bigger than she was.

The mailbox was full this morning; she had to unpack it like a suitcase. Two magazines, the *Friday Advertiser*, four catalogues, and a slightly squashed package addressed to the McDowells from the McDowells. Sending home the souvenirs, were they? Postmark: Quebec. Hanna studied the stamp enviously, trying to imagine what you bought in Quebec, what you saw there, how it would feel to just light out some morning for a place like eastern Canada, thousands of miles away. She'd never been out of western Oregon. To her knowledge. Of course, she might have traveled widely *without* her knowledge. Pre-Bessie. Pre-anything she could remember. She might have been born someplace else altogether—say, Quebec. Her mother a French-speaking native, red-haired and witty—her father a solitary wanderer, who'd chanced on this little hotel, and . . .

Oh, shut up.

She tossed the mail on the coffee table and stood a moment trying to think if there was something else she was supposed to do. In the silence she could hear the plaintive strains of the harmonica from the nether regions, still sounding lonesome. He must be feeling so, underneath—this was his fifth day on his own, cut off from his mom and everything he knew. Yet he was dead set against going back.

As she stooped to unplug the timer gadget and transfer it to another lamp, she wondered just how bad the situation was that he'd be going back to. It depended on My Mom, she supposed. Funny, he'd scarcely said a word about his mother. Why?

It seemed a pretty good question. Maybe she'd ask it. On her way upstairs to shift the other timer, she assembled some more good questions: What's your mom like, really? (Aside from "nice," his solitary comment so far.) What's she look like? Who do you take after, your dad or her? (And while we're on the subject, who do *I* take after? All guesses wel-

169

come, enter as many as you like.) How's she going to feel if you stay away?

And for all I know, Hanna told herself, trying not to hope for it, the answer to that one might be "good riddance."

By the time she got down to the art room the sad little tunes had stopped, and he was perched on the tall stool by the worktable, hunched busily over a sheet of paper.

"Writing a letter home?" she inquired.

He let that pass with no more than a patient glance. "Drawing Grandad's cow," he said. At once he added, "Listen, what *is* that machine thing? D'you know? And *that*." His pencil jabbed toward the nearest walls.

"The machine thing's a proofing press. A real old clunk." She went over to it and ran a vaguely affectionate hand over the rollers, switched the motor on and off briefly. "I used to know one of these monsters personally. We can run off a few religious tracts if you like—if they've got any type. Or how about some nice new twenty dollar bills?" That's my embezzler's blood talking, she thought. "The other contraption's an etching press," she went on, turning away hastily. "A thing artists use. So Barney tells me."

Jerry's inspection of the presses remained hostile. "Well, I liked this place better when it was a playroom. Who's Barney? Oh—the guy who lets you use his jeep."

And his shoulder to bawl on, she thought. Or he

would if I'd give in and bawl. "I didn't even know your grandad had a cow. He keep it in the front yard?" She leaned over his drawing, saw a much-corrected cartoon version of something that might be called a cow—a straight back view, with the head turned right around to glare at the onlooker with pin-dot eyes under curving horns. A laugh burst out of her; she stifled it quickly, with a side glance at him.

"It's meant to be funny," Jerry assured her. He examined his handiwork with a one-sided grin. "It's the only thing my grandad can draw. I can't even draw *it*. Is that Barney an artist?"

"Good lord no. He learned about etching presses from the far side of a broom."

"My mom used to draw me pictures when I was little," Jerry remarked, erasing his cow's tail and carefully making it thinner. "Not very good ones, I guess. But I thought so then."

Hanna seized her chance. "You never told me much about your mom," she remarked. Draped across a corner of the worktable, as if she had all day, she started casually, conversationally, down her list of questions, half expecting him to clam up right away. He didn't do that, but at first his answers were vague and reluctant. Oh, she was just a mom, he guessed. No, he didn't take after her—not in looks anyway, she was sort of blonde. Well, maybe in other ways, they both liked to read, if that's what Hanna meant . . .

He didn't know *how* to tell about his mom, she

realized. He couldn't get the perspective. She suspected too that he didn't want to talk about her—that he'd been trying hard not even to think of her the past few days. But as she probed, a picture began to emerge of a resolute but somewhat timid woman, who had found it hard to cope on her own these years since her divorce, who was over-anxious about Jerry, about his friends—though she tried not to be—who was devoted but unsure of herself as a parent, who badly needed the support and reinforcement of a husband however well she had managed so far.

And she had managed well; the more Hanna heard, the clearer it became that her guesswork as to the comfortable, well-ordered life he was envisioning in California was probably right on the button. There had to be a way to wake him up.

"Your mom's going to miss you if you don't go back," she murmured. Understatement of the century. There'd be no "good riddance" from this lady —there'd be an emotional disaster.

"I don't see why," Jerry stated in his most unyielding voice. "Nothing'll be the same now anyway. She's spoiled everything. Why did she want to go and get *married*? I was taking care of things for her, wasn't I? Listen, I even fixed the plumbing once! I can put on car chains, I can clean out gutters, I can smear stuff on that leak in the roof when it needs it. It isn't as though he was—my dad or something."

Hanna opened her mouth to say that might be

one of Walter Fox's great attractions, but closed it without speaking.

"Oh, well," Jerry finished, adding a row of angry-looking grass blades to his cow drawing, "she doesn't need me now. It's okay by me! Let Walter Fox do all that stuff."

"Walter Fox can't be her kid," Hanna said.

"So what. She'll have three new ones to make up for it."

Hanna sighed. The more she pushed, the harder he'd push back. This wasn't the way.

Jerry had flung aside his pencil and was staring out the big windows, half turned away from her, his cheek on one fist. For a while they were silent, following their separate mental paths. Then Jerry said suddenly, "It isn't as though I could go live with Dad. I mean, I would—I'd like to—if only Dad wasn't . . . well, the way he is." He swung around to glare fiercely into her eyes. "Why does he have to *be* like that? He's so great when he wants to be! Honest he is. But then when he *doesn't* want to be, he just forgets you exist! Just brushes you away like a fly or something. I don't get it!"

He was asking *her* why parents weren't perfect? All right, say something nice, she told herself. If you can think of anything. Or else say something mean enough to cut him free from that lousy bastard. She only wished she knew some good, surgically sharp words.

She made do with blunt ones. "Look, Jerry. Nobody can choose their parents. You drew one bum one—but it sounds to me like you drew a good one, too. Why not just concentrate on her, and brush *him* away like a fly? At least he's not a criminal, or a psycho, or a typhoid carrier or something."

"You mean—if he was, I'd never get to see him at all? He'd be in jail or somewhere like that?"

"Not just that," she said impatiently. She hadn't a doubt this kid would trot to the jail during visiting hours, probably bring along a cake with a file inside. "I mean you know who he *is*. That lets you know more about who *you* are—and what you aren't." Couldn't he see that? It was so plain. It was so *important*. It was a recurrent nightmare, knowing nothing of who came before you—what had gone into you.

He was quite unimpressed. "I don't see why. I hope I won't be *anything* like my dad."

She gave up. "Don't worry, you'll take good care not to be. You'll be different."

"Why can't *he* be different?" Jerry said dolefully.

"Oh, for God's sake! Come to the party!" Hanna exploded. "You can't change people! You can change yourself but you can't change anybody else, you have to take them just the way they come from the box! You little boob, you're *lucky*. You've got your mom and she's great. So write your dad off—just *scratch* him! Don't expect one damn thing from that man, now or ever! Then—" she grabbed him by the shoulders, gave him a fierce little shake, and sud-

174

denly hugged him hard. "Then anything you get is *gravy*. Don't you see?" She pushed him away, took a long breath. "And you don't keep *hurting*," she finished gently.

He was silent for some time, studying her face as if something important was written there that he couldn't quite make out. In a puzzled, oddly humble tone he said finally, "Well, I'll try." She endured another moment of scrutiny by those big, disconsolate dark eyes. Then he added, "You know what I think? I think you're lucky not to have any parents. That's what I think."

"Oh, come on, Jerry."

"I *do*. I bet if you had some you'd find out. You think foster parents bug you! Well, what makes you think real parents are any different? They bug you worst of all. Listen—" He poked a finger at her, warmed to his subject. "Supposing all at once you *found* yours. Your real parents. Maybe right when you had that thousand bucks saved up. Would you just drop everything and go live at their house, and be their kid?"

"Why, what are you talking about? I'd—" Jump at the chance, she was going to say, but didn't. Instead she said, "Oh, how do I know? That's got nothing to do with it." Silently she added, *I wouldn't, though. Not now. Couple of perfect strangers.* But you moron, she told herself, they wouldn't *be* perfect strangers, they'd be your parents. *Sixteen years late? They'd be strangers. And they'd be a drag.*

Jerry was saying, "Sure it's got something to do with it. D'you want real parents or don't you?"

"Okay, okay, so maybe I don't want 'em showing up at this point. I'd still like to know who they are! At least what they're *like*." That's really what I mean, she thought.

Oh, is it? she thought a second later. Maybe I only want to know what *I'm* like. And maybe that's quite different.

Jerry said something argumentative and went on proving his point, but she had stopped listening, being absorbed in a peculiar sort of Happening within herself, in which all her ordinary notions stood up and walked across her mind into new positions, forming totally unfamiliar patterns. *I only want to know what I'm like. What I'm made of—good stuff or trash.* Eventually she came to, aware that there had been a silence.

Jerry said crossly, "Well, you don't need to look at me like I *hit* you or something. All I did was ask a question."

"Yeah, and it's catching," Hanna muttered. She felt as shaken as if she'd been strapped to a pneumatic drill for the past thirty seconds. *All I want to know about is me. It's all I need to know about.* "Sorry, where were we? I guess I don't know any answers."

"Well, I'll tell you the answer," Jerry informed her severely. "You *don't* want to go live with them, they'd just let you down flat when you needed them most! Even grandparents let you down! They forget to let you know they've moved, or where their daughter lives, or anything else! . . . And if you can't count on your own family—"

"Try somebody else's," she finished with what she realized was unseemly frivolity. She was feeling a sudden desire to giggle, whether at herself, or Jerry, or this whole conversation, she wasn't certain. He sounded so world-weary, such a case-hardened veteran of suffering and betrayal—and he actually didn't know much of anything. She wondered if she did, either.

"Okay, if you think it's so funny," he said stiffly. "I'm hungry. I'm going upstairs and find some lunch."

Oh, lord. Now she'd torn that tissue-paper armor of his, and she had to mend it, it was all he had. She steadied him as he slid off the high stool and got his balance, then kept hold of him, waiting till he met her eyes. "Jerry, let me tell you something," she said gently. "I *don't* think it's funny. I don't think *you're* funny. But don't give up on the world. There's plenty of nice people in it, honest—like you, for one. Things look rotten now but they'll shape up. And someday—you may not believe this, but *someday* you're going to find somebody you can count on, somebody—" She broke off. "—somebody you can trust," she finished dazedly. What am

I saying? she asked herself, dumbfounded. Good lord, if Barney could hear me now.

But Jerry only said, "I already have." As she refocused on him, encountering an unwavering dark gaze, he added, "Haven't I?"

He means me, she thought. Me, he's talking about. And California.

For an instant she wasn't there on Sandpiper Road at all but at Mrs. Thomas's, a hundred miles south and eleven years back, when she was five and her life was filled with a Big Girl named Amzie Morris. Big girl—she might have been Jerry's age. But she was a lot bigger than a skinny five-year-old, and she was calm and square and not afraid of anything. A solid rock. For all Hanna knew, Amzie was solid rock between the ears, too, but at five you didn't care whether your idol was priceless ivory or merely bonehead, so long as she stood there and let you hang on when you needed to.

That's what Jerry wanted—a solid rock in his shifting life. It wasn't that she didn't understand. But a solid rock, according to any unbiased definition, would now stand squarely in the way of everything he was counting on her to do. Not to mention everything she wanted to do herself. Try and get him to see that.

This is too hard, she thought blankly. I can't solve this. Nobody could solve this.

"Hanna?" said Jerry.

"Okay, okay, what's the big rush? I like to stand around and stare sometimes. Did I tell you I brought some library books? One science fiction, and one—"

"You never answered my question."

"I'm not going to. Let's see you manage those stairs if you're so good at it. Here's your cane, pappy." She handed it to him, waved him away. "Go on, I've got to lock up."

She swung away from him and crossed the room toward the big window, whistling loudly. Even so, she heard him mutter, as he started hitching up the steps, "Okay, but I'll just ask you again tomorrow."

With a yank of the cord she brought the Venetian blind rattling down, abruptly plunging the room into gold-and-blue striped shadow. Then, suddenly weary, she slowly locked and bolted the outside door, and stood a moment leaning her forehead against the cool painted frame.

I cannot solve this goddam problem, she told herself firmly.

She wished she really wanted to solve it. Then maybe she could. But what she really wanted was to give in and do what they were both dying to do, the hell with whether it was best for either of them or not.

Jerry yelled, "I'm already up! You coming?"

Automatically she started toward the stairs, as if he had her on a long line. Yes, she was coming. And unless she passed some sort of miracle by tomorrow they were probably going. It looked like Strike Three.

It couldn't be.

Think, she ordered herself. There's got to be a way. *Find* it.

NINE

—◆—

Jerry was glad of the library books, because soon after lunch Hanna left and didn't come back on the bicycle at all Friday afternoon, or after supper either. Not a word about it, she just didn't come.

He read the books and tried not to feel wounded —or sulky, either, like some spoiled-rotten baby who had to have what he wanted or else. As the evening passed he found himself trying not to feel it was *his* fault. But by Saturday morning he knew it was. He'd just bugged her to death, that was all. Argued and needled and never let a chance pass to put the pressure on a little harder. And she'd got so sick of it—and him—that she'd just stayed away. He wondered, as he ate his cornflakes—which tasted like papier-mâché this morning—whether she'd even come today. He couldn't honestly blame her if she didn't.

He washed his bowl and spoon and hobbled into the living room to peer out the front window, which showed him the same stubbornly empty street as the kitchen window had. He hobbled back into the kitchen, opened the breezeway door, and listened, hard, for what was probably a full minute and seemed like hours.

Gulls. A little wind, in gusts. The ever-present breathing and mumbling of the ocean. No jeep.

Well, what did you expect? he asked himself angrily as he limped back into the living room and picked up the practical knots book again. Why'd you have to act that way, anyhow? It's not as if there was any chance of talking her into it. You *know* you can't. You've known all along she'll make you go home. Sooner or later. It's just a matter of time.

He flung himself into one of the leather chairs, which snorted like a surprised horse, and reluctantly let himself think about home. It was like letting your tongue feel its way once more into the hole left by an uprooted tooth, like touching gingerly the very edge of a boil. It hurt, with a familiar, somehow addictive sort of pain that kept making you do it again just to see if it still felt that way.

It still felt that way. Sore, and tangled, and hopeless. How could he go back? There was a mountain in his way. A mountain of problems and ways and means and shrill questions and loud answers and reproaches and guilt feelings and humiliations and no privacy and yelling matches and inward despair and hating people and longing for people and . . . A whole mountain of pure barbed wire, with no way through.

He took a long, shaky breath and opened the practical knots book, groping in his pocket for the cord. If Hanna wouldn't go to California with him he'd just go alone. As far as his bank account and the state police would let him. Providing he could find motels that would rent a room to a kid . . . Forcibly he shoved all that to the back of his mind and got busy with his knots.

They occupied half an hour or so. By then he'd had it with sitting still, ankle or no ankle. He hauled himself out of the chair, limped into the hall, hitched upstairs just for the practice—and the exercise—hitched back downstairs. He was starting for the other stairs and the lower deck when he heard in the distance a well-known growl, which grew rapidly louder and more certain. Relief flooded over him. He was already halfway to the kitchen, whispering, "Oh, *thank* you!" to nobody in particular, when the jeep turned into the drive.

The instant he saw Hanna he knew something was different. It stopped him dead in the doorway. "What's happened?" he breathed.

For a moment she just looked back at him, with no special expression that he could translate, but with something strange about her that he could feel through every pore. It was as if she had kept her same skin but turned into something radioactive inside. At last she swallowed—he could see her throat ripple—and said, "Happened?"

"Yes, happened! Something's happened. Did you get fired? Did—somebody find out?"

"No, no, no, relax."

"But then what *is* it?" His heart was beginning to beat hard and fast.

"Something nice." She turned away swiftly and dumped her purse on the counter, tossing the broken strap up over it, then faced him again, her eyes bright but her smile a bit stiff. "It's simple enough. You've won."

It didn't mean a thing to him at first. Won what? Then it exploded in his brain. "You mean I—you mean we—"

"I mean we're going. I give in."

He tried to yell, but nothing came out, and there was a kind of commotion going on inside him, with thoughts and feelings flailing confusedly, like survivors splashing around a capsized boat. Hanna grabbed his arm, saying in a much more Hanna-like tone of voice, "Maybe I should've made you sit down first. What did you *think* I meant? We've only been fighting one battle that I know of."

"But I never—I never really thought—expected—"

"You never thought I'd come around?" Still gripping his arm, she turned him toward the living room, flashing him a side glance. "Counting on that, were you?"

"Of course I wasn't!" he protested. But I was, he thought numbly. I guess I *was*. Otherwise, why did he keep having this unbalanced, upside-down feeling, as if a chair had been jerked out from under him? Realizing that he was leaning heavily on Hanna he scowled and pulled his arm free. "You don't need to help me! I can walk just fine. What made you change your mind?"

"Oh—things. You. I don't know, I just did." She peeled off her windbreaker and tossed it on the window seat.

"You might've told me sooner! You could've come back yesterday afternoon or—"

"I only decided last night. About three o'clock in the morning. But since then I've got it all worked out. Come on, sit down. I'll tell you."

Dry-mouthed and feeling oddly unreal about everything, he obeyed, telling himself they were *going*, it was *happening*. Briskly she began to outline her plan, ticking off points as she made them by pushing back the supple, freckled fingers of her left hand with the forefinger of her right. There were certain things they needed; one, money; two, a destination; three, transportation; four, a good lie to cover her sudden departure from Cotters'; five—

"You mean you're not going to tell the Cotters? Or the agency? I thought you said it was okay when

185

you were sixteen, and they wouldn't mind, in fact they'd be glad to—"

"They will. It is okay. I'll write the agency—the letter'll get there Monday. But I don't want Barney to know I'm going till I'm gone. Where was I? Five —a plan for leaving town separately or anyhow making it look that way; six—"

"We have to leave town separately? But—"

"Wait," she commanded. "Six, new names that sound like real names, not Smith or Jones; seven, a story we can get down pat and stick to when anybody wants to know what the hell we're up to. A story without holes. Okay. Now. We'll leave on Monday—"

"*Monday?* We can't wait till Monday, we—"

"Jerry, if you keep interrupting I'll never get through explaining in time to leave at all!"

"Yes, but my *mom* gets home Sunday, remember? That's tomorrow! And she'll find out I'm gone and she'll start hunting and—we'll have to go tomorrow morning, early! Or *today!*"

"Okay, great. Now tell me how we get our money out of the banks on a Saturday or Sunday."

"Oh. Yeah." Jerry took a long breath and subsided. "Okay, go on."

"We leave on Monday, as soon as we can after the banks open. That'll be somewhere around ten-fifteen. But there aren't any buses then. There's one at eleven-ten, going to Coos Bay and Brookings,

186

and one at ten-forty going to Grant's Pass and Med-
ford and on down to Sacramento."

"That's the one, then!"

"Well, I don't know." Hanna studied her finger-
nails a moment, frowning. "That one seems so obvious. I mean, anybody'd know we were heading for
California. I thought maybe if we went to Coos Bay,
then got off the bus and maybe hitchhiked over to
the I-5 at Roseburg, and got another bus there—
maybe even thumbed on down to Grant's Pass and
then to Eureka . . . What d'you think?"

Jerry swallowed. It seemed a lot of—riding with
strangers. His mother's face rose up before him—his
Scoutmaster's—even his dad had warned him never,
never . . . He pushed all the faces away. Hanna
knew what she was doing. "I don't know, I've never
hitchhiked," he said as casually as he could. "You
don't think I'd be kind of—noticeable? With my
cane?"

"Oh, no, kids break legs and things all the time.
We'll say you fell out of a tree. Nobody'll think
twice about it. So anyway, there we are in Eureka
and it's probably time to get a hamburger and a
motel. A real el-cheapo, it'll have to be. And it'll feel
like it."

"Oh, *that's* okay. I've slept in a sleeping bag lots
of times. Outdoors, on a *rock*."

"Then you'll feel right at home."

"But listen, Hanna. If we took that other bus in

187

the first place we'd be *lots* farther away in lots less time, wouldn't we? If we fool around standing at the edge of I-5 with our thumbs up . . . a kid with a cane and a red-haired girl—*you're* kind of noticeable yourself, don't forget."

"I'm going to wear a ski cap. Don't you worry about me. I've even got my lie for the Cotters set up already. I told Mrs. Cotter I might go down to Tilla-mook next week, to see Marianna Weber—that's another foster kid I know, she lives on a dairy farm down there somewhere. I don't know where, but it doesn't matter. All I need is a reason to be gone on Monday with a suitcase."

"What'll you tell Samantha?"

"Nothing. She'll find out soon enough."

Jerry studied her closely a minute, struck by a slight change in her voice, he couldn't tell what. "Will you—be sorry you quit your job? Afterwards? It's such a good job."

"Naa, I'll get another one. I'm a cinch at getting jobs. I've worked all kinds of places. What d'you think our name ought to be? I was wondering about Jenkins, maybe. You like that?"

"*No.* I know a kid named Tony Jenkins who's a drip. What about Abernathy?"

"Kind of fancy. Brown. How about Brown? Or Green. Or White."

"Or Purple," said Jerry. Abruptly, he giggled. All at once they were both giggling uncontrollably, whooping with laughter, falling around on the window seat, helplessly pounding their knees. Jerry felt himself almost sobbing once, and made a desperate effort to sober up, then went off into another gale before he could make it. But finally they were over it, wiping their eyes and beginning to catch their breath, and he was surprised to notice that he felt better—relieved, somehow, not so keyed up and scared. All at once it began to be exciting and marvelous fun. "Let's find a name in the phone book!" he suggested.

They settled at last on Snodgrass, as being the sort of name everybody had heard but nobody would think you chose on purpose. Jerry decided to be Charles Mark Snodgrass—which he liked far better than his own Jerome Harold—and Hanna insisted on being Angelica Ann.

"*Angelica?*" Jerry repeated incredulously.

"You can call me Angie—everybody can. But *I'll* know I'm Angelica Ann. What's the harm in that?"

"Well, okay. Then I'll be Mark. Angie and Mark Snodgrass, and we're brother and sister? What about our folks? Both dead?"

"We're *half*-brother and sister. That's how come we don't look anything alike." (Oh, that's *smart*, Jerry thought admiringly.) "And my mom died when I was two years old, but yours only died last spring. But our dad's been divorced from her for a long time, and lives in Quebec, we don't even know where."

"Where did *we* live? Before California?"

"Seattle," Hanna said firmly. "We don't want anybody nosing around where you *really* come from —and anyhow, Seattle's bigger than Portland and farther away. Nobody could check us out in a place like that. So after your mom died we decided we'd better move down to California where we had some cousins—actually they were *my* mom's relatives, yours was an orphan and didn't have any."

"What are their names?"

"*I* don't know. They can be Smith or Jones or something. Whoever they are they moved away long ago, only we didn't know it because we'd never kept in touch anyhow."

Something occurred to Jerry. "Listen, Hanna—if anybody really wanted to check us out in Seattle they could just look at all the school enrollments, couldn't they? We'd've been going to school some-place all last year."

"Oh, well." Hanna waved that away. "We don't even need to tell this story unless somebody asks us, and who's going to be asking us a lot of questions?"

"Our friends, maybe. I asked *you* a lot of questions."

For a moment her green eyes studied him enigmatically. Then she said, "So maybe we better not make any friends. Just keep smiling and clam up. Sort of keep to ourselves."

"Well—okay," Jerry said, though it seemed a hard thing to manage at school, where you got to know people whether you were trying to or not. Of

190

course, if he didn't go out for any teams or Debating Club or anything, and didn't have Scouts, and came right home after his last class . . . He realized he had no picture of the home he'd be coming to, or even where it would be. "Hanna, where are we going, anyhow? You never said."

She shrugged. "Wherever I can get a job. Feeding those elephants, you know."

"What'll you be doing really?"

"Likely waiting tables in some fast-food joint—or a cocktail bar, if I lied a little about my age. Or making beds and scrubbing out johns in a motel. That's the likeliest."

Jerry stared at her. "But Hanna!" Maybe she was kidding him, he hoped. But she only waited, eyebrows lifted inquiringly. "That's not a very good job, is it?" he said uneasily. "The motel one? I mean, that's hardly any better than shucking crabs."

"Well, making beds all day is hard on the back, and shucking crabs is hard on the hands. They probably pay about the same. And smell a little different." She finally did grin at him.

"You're just kidding," he said in relief.

She turned quickly, the grin gone. "Oh no I'm not. Not for one red-hot minute. I'm dead serious."

"But—Hanna, d'you *want* to make beds and scrub johns all day? I mean—"

"*Want* to? Now who's kidding! I just said that was likeliest. You gotta take what's available. I'll try for cocktail waitress first, that's good pay, counting

191

tips. Of course it'd mean working nights—or anyhow evenings, about four p.m. to midnight, something like that. We might not see much of each other." She gave a laugh and a shrug and stood up. "I'd better do my chores. Sit still, we can talk while I work."

For the moment Jerry had nothing to say. He sat appalled as Hanna headed for the kitchen, whistling —apparently unaware of the dismaying images she was conjuring up. If she worked late, she'd have to sleep late; he'd have to creep around being quiet, find something for breakfast and go off to school without waking her . . . stay at school all day clammed up, trying not to make friends or get to know anybody . . . come right home afterwards—to some place he couldn't even picture yet—with no activities—no bike—and Hanna would already be at work. Get his own dinner. Do his homework. Go to bed. And she still wouldn't be home. Get up next day and do the whole thing over.

Oh, well, she probably won't get that job, she said so, he told himself hurriedly. But he hoped it wouldn't be the motel job, either—he hated that idea. *She'd* hate it. She ought to have a job she'd like, something that would—get her somewhere. With promotions and raises and things. Only . . . maybe there weren't any better jobs for somebody who hadn't finished high school and didn't know how to type or—

192

"Can you type?" he asked her as she went past with the watering pot.

"Oh, sure." She gave a short laugh. "About fifteen words a minute. I've had one semester. I was going to take another crack at it this fall. Not to worry. I can pick that up on my own any old time."

Without any typewriter to practice on? Jerry thought.

The heretical idea crossed his mind that Hanna might be a little impractical. Some people just were —his mom, for instance. Now *he* was a practical type. Everybody said so. His mom was always saying *why didn't I think of that* and *I don't know what I'd do without you* ...

She was going to have to do without him now, he reminded himself with a sort of sickening free-fall sensation. Maybe Vicky could be practical for her.

Angrily he swept his mind clear and got up, grabbing for his cane. "Let me feed the fish, okay?" he said loudly.

"Sure, if you like. These plants still don't need water, if you ask me. I'm going out to get the mail."

The point was, Jerry told himself carefully as he got the fish food out of the end table drawer, he was maybe going to have to be practical for *Hanna* now. Tell her things that might not work, that might not turn out exactly the way she was counting on. And make sure she didn't get herself stuck in some job she just hated but didn't dare quit—because then she'd start hating *him*, for badgering her into this . . .

"I never saw anybody get so many catalogues!" she exclaimed as she came in the front door and pushed it shut behind her with one foot. "Clothes, cooking pots, calculators, *weathervanes*, for heaven's sake . . . Hey, I thought of a good name for our long-lost cousins who moved away before we could get there. Twombly! How's that grab you? Myrtle and J. Edgar Twombly . . . I can see that's going to strain you a little. What about Tuttle?"

"Hanna," said Jerry. "I was wondering—what kind of place will it be, where we live? Like a real small house, maybe? Or just an apartment?"

"*Just* an apartment?" Hanna looked up from the mail she was sorting to stare at him. "Jerry, it'll be a couple of rooms somewhere. I'll be lucky to swing that, on what I'll be making. But we'll try to get two connecting, and we'll get a hot plate in, so we can warm soup, and cook eggs and stuff like that. It'll be okay."

"Oh, yeah," Jerry said faintly, then, louder, "Sure! It'll be just great!"

Hanna went on studying him a moment, then dropped the rest of the mail and came over to stand in front of him, face to face. "It won't be like your house, Jerry. It won't be like your life. But *I won't walk out on you, either*—the way your mom did."

It was Jerry's turn to stare. "My mom didn't walk out on me!"

"What else do you call it? She went and got married, didn't she?"

"But that doesn't mean—that isn't—wouldn't change how she *felt* about me."

"I thought you said—"

"I never said she wouldn't *feel* the same! I said everything *else* is changed! She'd still—you know. Love me. Whatever happened."

"Oh. Sorry." Hanna shrugged, raised her eyebrows. "But you said—now she'd have Vicky and Tom and the other one, whatever her name is, and—"

"D'you think she'd ever like them as much as *me*?" Jerry demanded. He could feel the blood rushing up into his neck and face, throbbing in his ears. "If you think that, you're just crazy!"

"Okay, okay! I'm sorry! I'm only repeating what *you* said, I don't even know your mom!" Hanna made fly-shooing motions around her head, stalked out to the hall and upstairs.

Jerry glowered after her. No, you don't know my mom, he thought, at first angrily, then with that falling-through-space sensation again. She'll still love me no matter what. What's more she'll probably still need me—to help cope with Tom and everything. To be on her *side*. And she didn't walk out on me . . . I walked out on her. Anyway I'm about to.

After a while he came out of himself enough to

realize that he was standing beside the open drawer with the fish food box in his hand. Upstairs, he could hear Hanna walking here and there, whistling. He started to move, felt a painful twinge in his ankle, and thought he had never been so tired of anything in his life as he was of that ankle. It seemed a burden as big as the world. Everything seemed a burden as big as the world, even breathing and having to feed the fish. Slowly he creaked over to the fish tank, leaning on his cane like an old man, scattered a careless pinch of their dandruff over the water, creaked back to put the box away. Probably he'd given them too much, now, and they'd overeat and die. He hoped they did, he hated them, he wished they were dead.

No, of course he didn't wish they were dead, poor dumb things, what had *they* done? He limped back hastily to the tank and scooped out what he could see of the banquet still on the surface, though the banqueters were dashing and flashing about so enthusiastically it was hard to tell if there was much left over or not. He tried to care one way or the other and couldn't. He wished he hadn't tied his shoe this morning, even loosely. It hurt. He hurt all over. He sank down on the window seat, yanked the lace loose and painfully eased off the shoe, then stretched that leg out on the seat and lay back, the good foot still on the floor, his wrists crossed over his eyes. He wished *he* were dead.

Five or ten minutes later Hanna trotted downstairs again, and did something in the hall long enough for him to sit up quickly and get an ordinary kind of expression on his face before she came in the room.

"So. That's finished for today," she said briskly, but he noticed she flashed him a glance, probably to find out if he was still mad at her. He smiled to show her he wasn't, and after a moment's hesitation she smiled back, and sat down beside him. "Only one more day and the goldfish are on their own, right?"

"Yeah, right!" Jerry said.

"And look, I've got to leave before lunch, because Barney needs his jeep. I'll try to get back later but—maybe you better not count on it. I've got quite a bit to do before we take off. You understand?"

"Oh, sure!" Jerry said.

"Okay, Buster. I mean, *Mark.*" She laughed and stood up. "We better start getting used to it."

"Yeah—Angie," Jerry said. He sort of laughed too.

"Well. I'm on my way. There's a new jar of peanut butter, and plenty of bread."

"Yeah, I know. I'm not even—hungry yet."

"Okay. Well. So long, then. See you tomorrow."

"So long."

Still she lingered, as if something wasn't quite settled. He held the smile. Then abruptly she waggled her fingers at him and was gone. He waited till the jeep's familiar rumble faded in the distance before he let his face go slack and his body limp, and flung himself down on the window seat and gave up to panic.

How could he go to California? How *could* he, possibly?

He'd never really thought Hanna would let him. He'd never thought it would be *up to him.* But it was. He was right on the edge of walking out on everything—forever—and nobody was going to stop him.

He couldn't do it. He didn't *want* to. He had to go home, where else? He'd known it from the beginning.

He never liked remembering that afternoon, later. Most of it he spent outdoors on the lower deck, sitting on the steps in the uncomfortably chilly sunshine because he felt he could not stand to look at the goldfish and the leather chairs and the mail-stacked coffee table another minute. So instead he looked at gulls and grass and ocean and a heaped-up tangle of blackberry vines and a couple of small, busy birds. Mostly he looked inward at his shipwrecked thoughts and emotions, very few of which had found anything yet to cling to. The whole wonderful adventure had just fallen to bits in the moment of coming true.

There were at least a million things wrong with it, and he saw them now with noonday clarity. What he couldn't see was how he'd overlooked them before.

Imagine leaving his mom without a word, letting her come home all happy and find he'd just vanished into space, nobody knew where—why, it would be like taking a club and smashing her head in. He didn't know how he'd ever thought he could do it. He didn't know how he'd ever thought *any* of this would work—for Hanna, for him, for anybody. He hadn't *thought*, that was the answer. He'd just dreamed on, babbled on like Tom at his worst, waiting for Hanna to shut him up and find him a real solution. Instead she'd accepted his—if you could call it that.

Maybe there wasn't one. In any case, this wasn't it. To take off somewhere on your own and make a go of it, you needed a lot more than just a bank account. He saw that now, twenty-four hours too late.

As midday crawled toward afternoon he began to wonder if it was really entirely too late. Maybe it was more like one of those dreams where you're falling off a cliff and you wake up just before you hit the ground. But he had to wake Hanna up too. And he wished somebody would tell him how he was going to do that.

What would he *say*? "Oh, by the way, I guess I don't want to go after all." Terrific. When he'd talked her into it himself, argued and begged and *insisted*. That was going to be a great moment. He could hardly wait. There were lots of great moments ahead of him. Because his mountain of barbed wire was still right where he'd left it—a barrier between him and home as high and wide and tangled and thorny as that blackberry thicket at the edge of the yard. Just plain impossible. Impassable. Except to those stupid little birds, which kept popping in and out of the mess whenever they took a notion, as if they didn't know it was there.

After another moment of helpless staring, Jerry found himself actually watching the birds, and even leaning forward to observe one of them more closely. He was ready by now to take advice from anybody, even a dumb little bird.

Maybe it wasn't so dumb. It hopped over the first strand of vine it came to, stopped to jerk its head this way and that, peering all around, hopped a little to the left and ducked under some thorns, fluttered across a tiny clear space, then ducked again, veered right and hopped over a couple of strands . . . by now Jerry could barely see where it was by its movements; in another minute it would be hidden, still safe and sound, still moving right along.

Jerry straightened, blinking. Maybe the bird had a nest in there, maybe it just liked to hop through brambles to show it could, but it really had the technique down. He wondered, wearily, if there was anything in that for him.

To postpone thinking about it he got up, stiff with sitting in the chilly breeze, managed the four steps to the deck by clinging to the rail, then limped along to the art room. Once inside he remembered he'd never eaten any lunch, and labored on up to the kitchen. As he slathered peanut butter on a slice of bread and stood on one foot, leaning on the counter and chewing, he let his mind drift back cautiously to the bird.

One strand at a time. That worked fine if you were a bird, in a blackberry thicket. But with his barbed wire mountain? He'd thought of it as a solid mass, but he supposed there were individual strands, separate problems. He could even name some of them. For instance, how to tell Hanna he wasn't going. And how to get to Portland with no money. How to tell his mom where he'd been—*whether* to tell her. How to explain his ankle and the bandage and the cane. How to behave with Dad next time he called. How to get used to Tom living in his room, and Walter Fox being his boss, and—

Wait a minute. *One* strand at a time, not forty.

Jerry used his cane to drag the kitchen stool close enough to perch on while he finished his bread and peanut butter and slowly sipped a glass of milk. He was beginning—just barely—to grasp how the bird's technique *might* work for him, if he were patient and very, very careful.

At ten sharp Sunday morning the jeep turned into the drive. Jerry was waiting in the kitchen, tense but committed. Strand number one was How To Tell Hanna, and there was only one way: straight out.

She came in the back door, slung her purse on the

washing machine, stalked through the dog room and into the kitchen and saw him—and stopped with her mouth already open to say "hi." Instead she stood silent, wary, waiting.

In a voice he just managed to keep steady, he came out with it. "Hanna. I can't go. With you to California. I have to go home."

For an instant she didn't move and her expression scarcely changed. Then she sagged against the counter, forehead in hands, as if every bone in her body had gone limp on her.

It was far worse than Jerry had expected. "Oh, I'm *sorry!*" he cried, his voice completely out of control. "I'm *sorry!*"

"No, no." She was up off the counter as swiftly as she'd dropped there, and hugging him hard. "It's okay, Jerry. Honest. I understand."

"How *can* you?"

"Take my word. I do. Come on, let's go sit down before we fall down."

They did, flopping into the wheezing leather chairs and slowly sinking to the bottom as they searched each other's faces. Hanna's was sad but enigmatic, her expression too complicated for him to figure out. She seemed even paler than usual.

"Okay, give," she told him. "I want to know what changed your mind."

He told her, as well as he could. It was harder to explain than it was to think about, mostly because it was embarrassing to talk about love, and how he felt about his mom. It seemed too private, even for Hanna. And he hated to hurt her feelings by mentioning how that new life she'd described had sounded to *him*. He did say he thought it would be lonesome. "We'd hardly even see each other. And we wouldn't know anybody else. I just don't think it would work."

"I expect you're right, Jerry."

"Even for *you*. I mean—it's none of my business. But I think you ought to have a better job, not just . . ." He stopped. It *wasn't* any of his business. Not now. "But listen, Hanna. I want you to have the money, anyhow. If you're still going. I really mean it." Frowning at his hands, he waited.

Finally she said, "I know you mean it. But I refuse. N.O." He glanced up swiftly—she was smiling a little, and there was actually a pink tinge to her cheeks and chin and forehead. It was very becoming. "I wouldn't want to go without you," she added.

He smiled back, ashamed of the wave of relief flooding through him. He *had* meant it. But he hadn't known how he'd ever explain it to his mom. "I do think it'd be better if you finished high school first—and learned to type," he said earnestly.

"I expect you're right," she told him again.

Something—a mere flicker—in her voice or her eyes made him study her a moment. "Did you know it all the time?" he said.

"Yeah. But I didn't want to admit it either."

He nodded and leaned back in his chair, feeling a few of his muscles and nerves and things relaxing, just a little. Strand one was behind him. So far, okay.

After a minute Hanna said, "Well, we'd better start making new plans."

Jerry sat up again. "I've been doing that all morning. There's a bus at eleven-forty-five—today. I called. The only thing . . . I'll have to borrow ten bucks from you. I'll mail it right back," he added hastily. "Our neighbor owes me lawn-mowing money. I'll send it here—to this house—addressed to A.A. Snodgrass." He waited till she answered his smile. "So you watch for it. I bought just a one-way ticket coming down, see. I thought Gran—"

"Relax, I've got ten bucks. But how're you going to get from the bus station to your house?"

"Well—I was hoping—d'you think I could keep this cane?"

"Be my guest. I mean Grampa Cotter's guest. He's been dead three years, he'll never miss it. But Jerry, you can't *walk* to your house, can you? Even with a cane."

"No, but there's a sort of park only a couple blocks from the bus station. My dad drops me off there sometimes when we've been to the lake. I sit on the bench and wait for Mom to pick me up."

"But this time she won't be coming to—"

Jerry cut in swiftly. "I've—arranged that, too."

204

He didn't mention the bad half-hour he'd spent, taking the phone off the hook and putting it back again, limping up and down the hall, telling himself he wanted a drink of water first, better go to the bathroom. In the end he'd sat down and got it over with. The Fox kids were all there at the house already. He'd thought they would be; Aunt Carol had said something about coming straight there from early church. Vicky had answered. He'd been more or less hoping it would be Aunt Carol, but he'd decided beforehand to give the message to anybody who picked up the phone, and that's what he did. Just—would she tell his mother to collect him at the park any time after two-fifteen, and warn her he'd be walking funny because he'd twisted his ankle. It had all come out in a rush and he'd been ready to hang up as soon as Vicky said okay. But instead she said, "Oh! I'm sorry. Does it hurt very bad?"

"No, it's okay. It's almost well again," he muttered.

"But—I mean, at your dad's and everything. That's awful."

"Yeah, well, it didn't matter." He didn't know how to get off the phone. "Well—if you'll just tell my mom."

"I will. They're supposed to be here pretty soon." A pause, during which he said "Well," again, then all at once she said, in an odd sort of voice as if she were pushing herself to it, "Look, Jerry—about Tom. I mean, what he said about riding your bike.

205

You can forget it. He won't be doing that. You don't need to worry."

It caught Jerry entirely by surprise: he stuttered a moment and ended by saying he hadn't been worrying. What a lie. Of course he had.

Vicky said, "Okay—I just wanted you to know. I can handle Tom. I can keep both of them in line."

It took him a moment to grasp it. *I'll be on your side*, she was telling him. *We can be on the same side—if you'll have me. To keep the peace. To make it work.*

"Okay," he said slowly, answering what she hadn't spoken, rather than what she had. "It's a deal." He heard himself add grudgingly, "I guess he could ride it sometimes. Once in a while."

Now why did I have to say that? he asked himself in annoyance as soon as he hung up. He was thinking the same thing now, remembering, still annoyed but not sure whether or not he wished he could take the words back.

"Anyway," he said to Hanna, shrugging it aside, "I phoned, and Vicky's going to give my mom the word, so—What's the matter?" he demanded, catching sight of Hanna's face.

"You phoned Portland—from this phone, Jerry? Don't you remember—"

"Oh, sure, I remembered! I reversed the charges. I mean—not to our phone, because then my mom'd see the bill. I . . . I charged the call to Dad."

"To your *dad?*"

"Yeah." He watched her anxiously, hoping he'd figured that one right. "I just—told the operator I wanted to charge it to my father, and gave her the number and she said whose name is that listed under and I told her and she put the call through."

About halfway along he'd seen the laughter start far back in her eyes, which suddenly turned a lighter green, like sea-water in the shallows, and he, too, felt a smile tugging at the corners of his mouth. By the time he finished they were both grinning like idiots.

"Good—thinking—Buster!"

Jerry was a little proud of it himself. "Well, I knew he'd never notice. He has a secretary pay his bills. Anyhow, I sort of figured it was his fault I was down here in the first place."

"You're right. Jerry, I begin to have hopes of you. You might visit the jail. But no cake. No file."

"What?"

"Forget it." Hanna flapped a long-fingered, freckled hand and stood up. "Looks to me like you've got things all worked out. At least right up to climbing into your mom's car." She paused, deadpan again. "So what're you going to tell her?" she said casually.

"I don't know yet."

"You don't *know*? My God, hadn't you better—"

"I mean I'm not going to tell her *anything*—until she asks a question. And then I'm going to answer. Just that question." One strand at a time, Jerry reminded himself doggedly, clinging hard to the dumb little bird.

"But won't she be full of questions?"

"Why should she? She'll think I was at Dad's. And if the two of them act like usual they won't even talk on the phone for months. Especially now she's married."

"He won't call to—sort of explain where the hell he was?"

"He'll call me. When she's not there."

"I see." Hanna eyed him thoughtfully, hands in the back pockets of her jeans. "She'll ask about the ankle."

"Sure. I'll tell her the truth. I was climbing up a steep slope and slipped, and got my foot caught in some rocks. I don't need to tell who put the bandage on. She'll think she already knows."

"The truth, nothing but the truth, but not necessarily the whole truth—is that it?" Hanna was smiling a little, but she shook her head. "She'll find out something or other, sooner or later. Then she'll ask the right questions."

"Well, then I'll tell her the right answers." Jerry pulled in a long breath, promised himself once more that it *would* work, that he *wouldn't* panic. "Maybe —by then—she'll see why I did it. And she'll see I can take care of myself anyhow. Of course," he added, feeling rather deflated, "I guess I couldn't have, without you."

"Yeah, well, accidents can happen to anybody.

You were doing a great job before—and you're doing a great one now." Hanna glanced at her watch. "And we'd better get moving or you'll miss your bus. Or have you already packed too?"

"No—I was just starting—and shouldn't we wash my sheets?"

They both got moving, making sure Jerry had everything he came with, that everything he'd used or moved out of place or read was back where it belonged. Hanna stuffed sheets and pillow cases and towels in the washer and started it; Jerry watered the plants for her and fed the fish, then filled his backpack, which wasn't as fat as before. He wondered if his mother would ever miss that other pair of jeans. Finally Hanna went upstairs to reset the radio timer.

Eleven-fifteen. Just half an hour, and he'd be on that bus, and starting for home. He stood looking slowly around the living room that had once been Gran's and Grandad's and now was his and Hanna's. It was certain to be the last time he'd ever see it. He wondered if he'd ever even come to Horseshoe Beach again. Or ever again see— His thoughts stopped, as if they'd run into a brick wall.

Hanna came swiftly down again, took a last glance around, and said, "That's it. Here, I'll hoist that backpack up for you."

"Hanna," said Jerry. "D'you think we'll ever— see each other again?"

It must have crossed her mind long before it had

his, because she didn't even look surprised. "I don't think so, Jerry. I mean—I can't see how we'd go at it, can you? It'd never just happen by itself. And— we hope—nobody but us is ever going to know about this week."

"But—cripes *sake*—!"

Hanna cut him off short. "Listen, we can't have it both ways. Let's keep it the way it is—one week. One secret week."

He was silent, struggling to make his peace with that. In a moment he said, "Well anyway—when I'm a little older I can come down here by myself and see you. Whenever I—"

"Yeah, sure. Of course by then I might be gone. Here—" She fumbled among the stacked mail, pulled out a "Boxholder," found a pencil and handed them to him. "Write your address. Someday when I've got one of my own, I'll send you mine."

He swallowed, did as she told him, and handed her the card, which she stuffed into a pocket as she turned away, hauling the backpack by its straps.

"Okay. Let's go."

Numbly he followed her through the archway, across the hall. He stopped short as he remembered something else. "Hanna! The key to the deck door —the one that's supposed to hang on that key rack in the hall closet. I think I left it down there on the worktable."

"Leave it, I'll get it tomorrow. I've got to come back five more days, you know." She paused, looking at nothing and then, briefly, back at him. "Going to be funny—nobody here but the goldfish. Well, come on." Abruptly she slung the backpack onto his shoulders and made for the kitchen. In another minute they were out of the house, climbing into the jeep.

TEN

The bus was four minutes late—four of the longest minutes in Hanna's life. When she pulled into the parking lot of the Crab Pot Cafe, which served Horseshoe Beach as bus terminal, there was a small knot of people waiting beside the sidewalk bench, but not a sign of the Greyhound. By the time she'd parked the jeep in an inconspicuous spot underneath some trees, two more passengers had come out of the restaurant.

"It'll be here any minute," she told Jerry. "You better get on over there."

"Yeah." He put his hand on the door handle but didn't push. "Hanna—do I buy my ticket in the restaurant or on the bus?"

"I dunno. From the driver, I should think. Ask one of those people."

"Okay." He swallowed audibly, turned to her.

"No soppy stuff," she commanded. "So long. Keep your nose clean. Kick your dad for me when you get a chance."

He gave a strangled laugh, flung himself on her and hugged her hard. Then he banged the door open, slithered out, and banged it behind him. Head averted, he hunched the backpack into place and hobbled rapidly away. She watched without moving as he reached the waiting group, hesitated, then spoke to a grandmotherly looking woman, who smiled and gestured toward where the bus would be when and if it came.

And it better come quick, Hanna thought. In fact, why don't I leave? My mission's accomplished.

Silly question. She was tied to this spot, nailed to it, until that kid got on the bus and the bus pulled out. He had retreated to the edge of the group, eased his backpack to the ground, and propped himself against the back of the bench, leaning on Grampa Cotter's battered old cane. Something beautiful to remember me by, Hanna thought.

He was glancing around the waiting passengers, outwardly indifferent—to make sure nobody was watching, she knew as if she could read his mind. Then, still casual, he slowly turned until he was staring straight toward the jeep. They had agreed they wouldn't wave, she wouldn't get out, they would try to make it appear they were not together. But he had to look in some direction, didn't he? She draped her arms over the steering wheel, leaned forward until she knew her face was visible through the windshield, and stayed there, staring back.

Quite an act she'd put on yesterday. It made her wonder if she'd missed her calling, and ought to train for the stage. Or take up gambling. Lord, what a chance she'd taken—and gone home not knowing at all if she'd told umpteen big fat lies for nothing. But they'd worked. And today she'd won the prize. The booby prize. The Sunday School Bible for good behavior. At least, she'd won if that bus ever came and broke this eye-lock, this dotted line between her and that kid in the red shirt by the bench.

So what happens now, Ms. Holderith? she asked herself. Not to him, to *you*.

Back to wherever you left off last Sunday, what else? Back to plan A, and high school, and learn the damn typing. Or maybe take up drama. And keep your eye on that thousand bucks. Anyway he was probably right, and it's better this way. I've waited sixteen years, I can wait another one.

When was the bus going to show up? She snatched a glance at her watch. It was already past time. Unless this five-dollar wonder of hers was gaining again, which it probably was. She gave it a clout or two with the heel of her hand, and refocused her eyes on Jerry. Mustn't forget that key he'd mentioned. Downstairs on the worktable . . . She was suddenly visualizing something else that was prob-

214

ably still on the worktable—his drawing of Grandad's cow. Better check tomorrow. She hoped she was going to throw it away, if it was there. She hoped she wasn't going to *keep* it, forever and ever, like some damn silly lock of hair.

Thank God the McDowells would be home Friday. Only five more visits to that house. In fact, four. Samantha would probably do the last check.

There came the bus. Flickering into the corner of her eye, hissing and chuffing as it braked behind a car, sliding alongside the curb at last like a snub-nosed dragon and whooshing out all its air at once. The doors rattled open. The waiting group surged toward them, washed back slightly as the driver climbed down, shoving back his cap.

Jerry must have heard the noises, felt the stir. He didn't move, except to straighten so that he was no longer leaning on the bench. The dotted line never wavered. Behind him, the knot of passengers transformed itself into a straggling queue and began to file past the driver into the bus.

Go, Hanna told him fiercely. Buzz off. Get on that contraption and *leave.*

She saw him lift one hand three inches from his side, palm toward her. She raised hers into the windshield in a return salute. He turned abruptly and hobbled toward the bus, joined the last of the line and in another minute was inside.

And that was it. The driver resettled his cap, swung himself aboard, rattled the doors shut. The motor was still running. A few gasps and grunts and the behemoth nosed out into the traffic, ground into a higher gear, and became a receding object half-obscured by other cars—so fast, so *final*. Dear *God*. She wasn't *ready*.

Shut up, you'll never be readier, she told herself.

She unclenched her hands from the steering wheel, reached shakily to turn the key. She unclenched her jaw, too, only then realizing she'd been gritting her teeth so hard they ached. The jeep shuddered into life, reluctantly settled into its usual growl, and she backed and turned, pulled out of the lot and headed toward Pelican Avenue. Four more trips to the house on Sandpiper Road to feed those goldfish. She hoped she could stand it. She hoped Jerry would be okay. She hoped—she *knew*—she'd done right. She'd done *right*.

Unexpectedly, tears sprang to her eyes, an aching knot to her throat, a strange, bursting sense of relief into her mind.

Stupid, she thought, fumbling for a Kleenex and blowing her nose hard. Watch where you're driving. Nobody's walking off into the sunset to live happily forever after. Especially you.

On the other hand, she doubted she'd ever go back to quite where she was last Sunday. There'd been an important change—and she was having the oddest, most un-Hanna-like feeling that she wanted to tell old Barney all about it.

Because as it turned out, he'd been dead right

after all. She'd finally found somebody she could trust.

Herself.

And already, everything was beginning to seem different.